Hidden Emotions:
Family Ties, Family Lies

This book is a work of fiction. Names, characters, places and incidents are products of the author's imagination or are used fictitiously. Any resemblance to actual events or locales or persons, living or dead, is entirely coincidental.

ISBN 0-984702490
EAN-13 978-0-9847024-9-7
LCCN 2014920169

Hidden Emotions: Family Ties, Family Lies

a novel by

Paulette Jones

Editor

Paula Tromp

Your Time Publishing, LLC P.O. Box 872365 New Orleans Louisiana, 70187

Paulette Jones

Hidden Emotions:
Family Ties, Family Lies

A special thanks to my teachers

Your Time Publishing, LLC P.O. Box 872365 New Orleans Louisiana, 70187

Chapter One

O ne of the most challenging experiences of my life began when I found myself waking up in Charity Hospital, completely disoriented and without any memories of what had come before. As I blinked my eyes open, confusion enveloped me, and my gaze roamed the room in search of clarity. Almost immediately, I noticed a flurry of activity around me, figures moving quickly, voices urging me to stay calm and not to move. To my surprise, my body felt as immobile as the statue in Jackson Square. As I fought through the haze clouding my thoughts, I quickly realized that their urgent pleas were directed at me, as I was alone in the room.

With determined effort, I tried to push myself out of bed. In my mind, I imagined standing tall and looking down at myself, but the reality was that I could only manage to sit up using my arms for support. Leaning forward, I started to inspect my body, and that's when I noticed an unsettling array of wires and tubes connected to my wrist and chest. A wave of fear washed over me, igniting a strong desire to escape.

As I sat there, grappling for composure, an alarming beeping sound pierced the air. Turning my head, I traced the noise back to a heart-monitoring machine, and seeing it sent my anxiety into overdrive. The beeping gradually quickened, mirroring the rapid increase in my own heartbeat, and I began to breathe erratically. Dizziness descended upon me, and my head started to sway back and forth. The weight of my body seemed too heavy for my arms, making them shake violently, and I feared they might snap beneath me. Just when I felt I couldn't hold on any longer, someone embraced me and eased my head back onto the pillow. As I searched their eyes for answers, all I found reflected back was a shared concern.

Desperate to express the turmoil within, I tried to speak, but a sharp pain in my throat halted me. It felt as if I had swallowed shards of glass, and the discomfort was overwhelming. When the pain became unbearable, I instinctively reached for my neck, only to hear a nearby voice urgently imploring me to stay still and avoid causing injury. Gradually, my body began to relax, but my head continued to bob in a slow, uneasy rhythm. A glance downward revealed a wound stretching from my navel to my chest. While I couldn't quite see the extent of it, the sight was jarring. I fought valiantly to stay conscious, but the next thing I could recall was lying down again, surrounded by the familiar, rhythmic beeping.

As I lay there trying to open my eyes, I became aware of the familiar sounds of the hospital: carts rolling past, the soft discussions of health professionals regarding blood pressure and heart rates, and the warm reassurances offered to loved ones. This time, rather than being frightening, these sounds were oddly comforting. The beeping I had once found unsettling now created a calming rhythm, and I could feel my head gently rocking to the soothing beat. With each small effort, I felt my eyelids starting to part and wondered if anyone would notice that I was waking up.

Gradually, shapes and colors began to take form around me. As my vision sharpened, I was finally able to confirm that I was indeed in a hospital. A nurse approached, whom I would soon come to know as Nurse Vanassa, she kindly inquired about how I was feeling. Although I struggled to respond, the pain in my throat was a constant reminder of my condition. Understanding my difficulty, she raised her hand in a reassuring gesture, letting me know that it was perfectly okay not to be able to speak. She shared some comforting news that my wife had been informed about my return to consciousness.

In that moment, a question rushed through my mind,

Back? Back from where?

The realization struck me hard: I not only had no recollection of where I had been, but my memory of my life before this moment felt entirely erased. I desperately tried to summon an image of my wife, but her face eluded me. In fact, even her name felt lost in the fog.

Despite the confusion and discomfort surrounding me, I felt a glimmer of hope. I was not alone, there were caring people by my side, and even in the midst of uncertainty, I sensed that I would find my way back. The journey ahead might be daunting, but I was ready to embrace it with an open heart, knowing that the support of those around me would guide me through. This experience, challenging as it was, would ultimately become a testament to my strength and resilience. With each moment, I felt a determination to rediscover my past and to build my future, step by step, with courage and optimism.

In a whirlwind of emotions, anxiety washed over me as I found myself wondering how to greet the stranger who was about to walk through the door. Just as that thought lingered in my mind, the nurse announced that someone was here to see me. I looked up and saw a figure approaching, squinting to recognize her amidst the haze. My heart raced like a drum, echoing the anticipation in my chest. As she stepped into the light, a wave of familiarity rushed back, and suddenly everything clicked, I remembered her name: Layla is my wife.

Seeing her felt like the most exhilarating reunion, as if no time had passed since I last laid eyes on her. The sound of my heart monitor picked up speed, matching the excitement that filled the room. Layla approached me with such grace and warmth, placing her hands on mine, stroking them, and in that moment, a wave of calm enveloped me. We shared a peaceful silence, and when I glanced at her, I noticed tears glistening in her eyes. To lift her spirits, I offered her a gentle smile, wanting her to know that I was okay.

After a moment, Layla began to share updates about our loved ones. Her voice was a soothing balm, telling me that KJ was doing well and that Keith and Devell had reconciled. As she spoke, a cozy heaviness pulled at my eyelids, and despite my efforts to stay awake, I soon succumbed to the comfort of her presence. When I opened my eyes again, she had left, and a wave of sadness washed over me. I longed to ask her how I had landed in the hospital.

Later, the doctor entered and asked if I remembered anything. I could only shake my head in response, feeling a bit lost. She explained that I had suffered a heart attack and that I'd been in the hospital for three months, moving in and out of consciousness. It was hard to process; three months had slipped by without my awareness,

Three weeks after waking up from what Layla lovingly called my well-deserved getaway; I dove into rehabilitation. It was an eye-opening experience to realize how weak my muscles had become after lying idle for so long. Even simple movements felt like lifting weights, and raising my arms overhead was nearly impossible. Luckily, Layla was my unwavering support, coming to the hospital every morning to help soothe my aching limbs. Her rubdowns made a world of difference; without her, I would have battled to even sit up. Gradually, I managed to sit without assistance, and the next goal was to get out of bed and walk.

That first attempt to rise was a daunting challenge. It felt as if an enormous weight pressed down on my shoulders, and my body trembled unsteadily. I faced moments of frustration and doubt, but I made a promise to myself, I was determined to stride out of that hospital hand in hand with my wife.

Layla became my foundation. Her faith in me never wavered; she consistently reminded me that I could overcome this hurdle. With her gentle caresses and reassuring whispers, she brought me comfort and strength. On some mornings, I tried to impress her by sitting up quickly or speaking clearly, but inside, I often grappled with pain. Yet, I didn't want to show my discomfort around her. While Layla was a crucial part of my healing journey, I have to admit that the thought of the bedpan was a significant motivator. The dread that came with its arrival pushed me to get better faster, especially when I felt the nurse took far too long to return to empty it.

As I progressed, I entered the next phase of my physical therapy, which focused on rebuilding my speech and strength. I worked on standing with a walker while making humming sounds, and at first, I struggled; sweat dripped down my face as I grappled to stabilize my arms and legs. The simple act of humming sometimes felt insurmountable.

However, every time I began to doubt myself, I would glance at the bedpan in the corner and draw strength from the determination not to rely on it for long. My hard work paid off as I eventually built my endurance to stand for half an hour and speak words without pain or shaking.

With my progress, I began to hope that I might leave the hospital soon. I remember my first genuine question to Nurse Vanassa: I eagerly asked when I could go home. Her smile was warm, but she didn't respond, she just pointed down the hall. At that moment, I didn't quite understand, but I felt the fire within me grow even stronger. I was ready to prove that I could overcome every challenge.

This journey has been a rollercoaster of emotions, but with Layla by my side and a newfound determination, I know I can conquer whatever lies ahead. Every day brings me one step closer to recovery, and I am filled with hope for the future. The road may be long, but I am more than ready to embrace it, with Layla's love lighting the way.

The next day brought a bright spark of hope as Nurse Vanassa entered my room with an exciting new companion, a walker with wheels in the front. She set it by my bed and turned to leave, but I couldn't help but call her back.

When can I go home?

I inquired eagerly. With a warm smile, she pointed down the hall.

Once you can walk to the end and back, she replied, encouragingly. I thought to myself, that sounds easy, and confidently mentioned I'd be home in just a couple of days. She chuckled supportively, wishing me good luck on my journey.

My first priority was to tackle the bathroom, so I carefully perched on the edge of the bed and maneuvered the walker closer. As I began to rise, I faced an unexpected challenge, the walker timidly slid away from me. When I tried to move my feet, it felt like they were glued to the floor. In a sudden rush of panic, I called out for help, and to my relief, Nurse Vanassa hurried back into the room, with a smile on her face.

You really want to get out of here, don't you?

She reminded me that I should wait for assistance before embarking on my walking adventure and encouraged me to be patient as she went to prepare for my walker training.

Once an hour passed, Nurse Vanassa returned, ready for the next step in our journey. It's time for a little exercise. We'll start by walking to the door and back, she announced. I thought it was a funny way to begin, believing I could handle the whole hallway. But as I took my first steps, I quickly realized the challenge ahead. Nurse Vanassa was right there, physically lifting my legs with each step, as my brain and limbs seemed to be in a disconnect. The pain I felt was a reminder of my reality, but I pushed through. After what felt like ages, I glanced at the clock to see that forty-five minutes had passed, and I had only progressed about five steps. It was disheartening, but Nurse Vanassa reassured me, in a few weeks, I'll be jogging down the halls and out the door. Just imagining that filled me with hope, even though I knew I couldn't quite make it to the bathroom solo just yet.

During quiet nights, I began practicing my walking, taking tiny steps away from the bed and back again. One evening, feeling a sudden surge of strength, I decided I would try for the bathroom. Just ten steps stood between me and my goal. I took a deep breath and ventured toward the door. To my delight, I made it. Once inside, I sat down, convinced I could hear celestial melodies celebrating my triumph. However, despite my excitement, nothing happened. It was a bittersweet moment, celebrating my journey but realizing there was still a way to go.

The following morning, Nurse Vanassa came into my room and immediately noticed my absence from the bed. She rushed toward the door, and I called out, I'm in here, she swung the door open to find me sitting triumphantly on the toilet, with a bright smile, she simply closed the door again. When I emerged, she was perched happily on my bed, grinning from ear to ear. It's time to tackle the hallway, your next big step toward going home, she announced. I felt a rush of joy, but it quickly turned into a wave of daunted anticipation as I saw the long hallway stretching ahead, seemingly endless.

Every morning, Nurse Vanassa and I ventured down the hall together, sharing bits of encouragement, and by evening, my wife would join me for our walks. Slowly but surely, as the weeks passed, I transformed my journey. After two months of dedication and hard work, I finally accomplished my goal: I walked to the end of the hall and back. I had no idea at the beginning just how challenging this journey would be, but I emerged stronger, closer to home, and filled with gratitude for the support that helped me along the way.

Chapter Two

The day before my release, Nurse Vanassa delivered some surprising news: I was ready to leave the walker behind. At first, I couldn't help but think she was joking, after all, I hadn't yet attempted to walk without it. She clarified that while the walker would stay with the hospital, I had the option to try walking unassisted. Despite her encouragement, I opted to keep my trusty walker for my journey home the following evening.

As I was wheeled down the familiar hallway, emotions surged within me, and I felt tears prick at my eyes. A mix of confusion and gratitude washed over me as I realized how much I would miss the incredible hospital staff, especially Nurse Vanassa. Despite the challenges she had put me through, we had forged a genuine connection. I dreaded missing the chance to thank her and bid her farewell since she worked during the day shift. To my immense surprise, as I was pushed through the hospital's front doors, there she was, beaming with warmth.

Are you trying to sneak out without saying goodbye? she teased with a grin.

In that moment, I couldn't help but stand up and wrap my arms around her in a heartfelt hug. Thank you for being there for me. Your unwavering support made this journey possible, I whispered, my heart full of appreciation.

Her radiant smile said it all as I climbed into the car. As we pulled away, I caught a glimpse of her waving goodbye, and for the first time, I noticed the sparkle in her eyes and the gentleness of her smile that had seemed so elusive before.

The first morning back home felt utterly foreign. Lifting my body into a sitting position felt like a monumental task, and I worried I might be relapsing as every muscle ached and my limbs refused to cooperate. Panic briefly set in, and I called out for Layla. She rushed into the room, concern etched on her face. I imagine my body must have looked quite distorted because she quickly began to massage my neck, soothingly working her way down to my toes. With every gentle stroke, the tension and discomfort began to wash away, and soon enough, I managed to get out of bed and shuffle my way to the living room. It was a bittersweet realization: It was my first time moving without the walker, and yet I felt so weak, as if all my rehabilitation had evaporated overnight. With persistence and patience, I gradually regained my comfort walking around the house over the next few weeks.

Once I was home, my family rallied together to help make my recovery as smooth as possible. One sunny morning, Keith dropped by with an enthusiastic grin. He announced that it was time for me to bask in some sunshine, but I was filled with trepidation. However, I knew it was an essential step on my recovery journey. I grasped his arm tightly, and together we ventured outside. Just a block away, doubt crept in, and I thought I might need him to fetch the car. But instead, he slung my arm over his shoulder, exuding unwavering encouragement.

To my surprise, we made it all the way back to the house, despite my initial frustration, I promised myself I wouldn't go on another walk with him again. Yet, the next morning, he returned, brimming with determination. This time, when we reached the half-block mark, I felt a flicker of strength reigniting within me. Just as I was about to turn around, he suggested, Let's see if we can make it the whole block. A mix of disbelief and frustration washed over me as I vowed once more that I wouldn't walk with him again.

But the following morning, there he was, ready to guide me once more. Embracing the possibilities of my newfound strength, I decided to stop resisting and began following his lead. Before I knew it, we were walking three miles a day, it was exhilarating to witness my progress, reminding me just how far I had come and how important it was to embrace support and encouragement along the way.

One bright morning, Keith called to let me know he wouldn't be able to join me for our usual morning walk. Instead of feeling disappointed, I took it as an opportunity to walk KJ to school. The distance was similar to our typical route, so I was excited to stay active. I informed Keith that there was no need for him to come over so early anymore since I was getting my exercise walking with KJ.

As we strolled along, our conversation flowed effortlessly. KJ shared that his math teacher was his favorite because she made understanding numbers enjoyable, which helped him tackle his assignments with greater ease. We reminisced about our last crawfish boil, a true community event. KJ, who has a real passion for crawfish, eagerly asked when we could have another one. I promised him that once I was feeling better, we would prepare a feast big enough for the entire block, and I could see the excitement in his eyes. We also chatted about the Grambling State football team, my alma mater, and the approaching battle of the bands. KJ expressed his curiosity about whether we would be attending the game again since he had such a fantastic time last year.

Walking with KJ brought a sense of joy and clarity to my heart. Our conversation sparked memories that I hoped would help me piece together what had happened during my time away.

After weeks of these cherished walks, KJ unexpectedly halted at a bus bench and motioned for me to sit. Intrigued by his behavior, I complied, unsure of what was happening. He looked at me with intent and said,

You were with her.

His statement threw me for a loop, and I found myself at a loss for words, I didn't know what he was referencing. It dawned on me that it might relate to something during my absence. When I remained silent, he reassured me, that it was okay, and we could talk about it later, which left me pondering with curiosity.

After dropping him off at school, I began my walk back home, but suddenly, an overwhelming flash of images surged through my mind, like a film reel rewinding. I briefly glimpsed an airplane, a car service, my packed bags, and a hotel room, disjointed yet vivid snapshots. It clicked that I had been planning a trip to New Orleans, inspired by something Layla and KJ thought they saw at church. Questions raced through my mind: Did something significant happen while I was there? My efforts to recollect the details only led me deeper into confusion.

As I continued walking, I found it challenging to concentrate. I glanced behind me and realized that the path I had just traversed seemed foreign. It hit me; I was lost. My heart raced as I pressed on, hoping to trigger some memories. Images of various people and places flickered in my mind, and just when I felt like I might give-up, I heard someone call my name. Turning around, I saw Layla sprinting towards me, yelling, Dee, where are you going, and where have you been?

In that instant, it struck me that I had unknowingly walked right past my house. Layla enveloped me in a warm hug, expressing joy as if I had been gone for ages. I felt an overwhelming mix of laughter and tears as I realized I had been in my own neighborhood all along; familiar yet unrecognizable. Layla insisted I come inside to rest, noting that I didn't look well at all.

Once inside, exhaustion hit me like a wave. Sweat streamed down my face, and my knees felt weak as I staggered across the room. I hadn't fully grasped how drained I was, I had been wandering for hours.

I thought, what a morning it turned out to be, filled with unexpected turns and so much gratitude to find my way back.

After taking some time to rest, I opened up to Layla about my experience after dropping KJ off at school. On my way back, I felt a sudden emptiness in my mind that left me feeling disoriented and lost. I instinctively kept walking, wishing for a familiar face to help me reconnect with who I was or for clarity to return. It was perplexing to experience this blackout, especially when I believed I was making significant strides in my recovery. Layla, ever supportive, encouraged me to take a breather, suggesting that perhaps I was pushing myself too hard and needed to slow down a bit.

In the midst of my confusion, Layla reached out to my doctor. She reassured her that it's not unusual for someone who has gone through trauma to feel disoriented and that it's best for me not to be alone during these challenging moments. She also shared that when memories return, it can be a daunting process.

Curious and a bit apprehensive, Layla prompted me to recollect the last thing I remembered after dropping KJ off at school. This thought brought a wave of fear; my mind had likely tucked it away for a reason. Despite my efforts, I struggled to recall anything that might provide clarity. It was both frustrating and exhausting, but I recognized the importance of trying.

Seated on my bed, I suddenly felt a throbbing headache wash over me. Cradling my head in my hands and rocking back and forth, I hoped for some relief. As the headache gradually subsided, memories of my trip to New Orleans began to surface, along with snippets of dreams. I distinctly recalled KJ saying, that I was with her, and I couldn't help but wonder how he knew that, it didn't come across as a question.

I longed to share my New Orleans experiences with Layla, but everything still felt jumbled in my mind. I realized that, eventually, I would need to discuss this with my family and friends, believing that they could help me make sense of it all. As I continued to ponder, my thoughts began to whirl, and I gently laid my head on my pillow. Before I knew it, KJ was standing beside me. A strange sensation washed over me, almost as if I were in a dream. However, when he placed his hand on my shoulder, it became clear that this was real. It was a reassuring moment amidst the chaos, reminding me that I wasn't alone in this journey.

As I gazed into his eyes, it was clear that he was on the verge of expressing something important. However, after a moment, he turned and walked away, leaving me feeling a mix of curiosity and concern. I called out to him, asking if he needed anything, and he simply replied that he wanted to ensure I was alright. He shared that when I dropped him off, he sensed I wasn't feeling quite myself. Although he had contemplated walking me back home, he ultimately decided to remain at school. He felt a pang of guilt for leaving me alone when he sensed something was amiss. I reassured him that it was alright, as I hadn't even realized that I needed assistance.

Out of nowhere, he repeated, you were with her. He paused, looking at me expectantly, but when I didn't respond right away, he continued to hold my gaze before turning to walk away again. In that moment, I was puzzled by his departure. As time passed, I came to understand that he was giving me the space to process what had just transpired. Slowly, the memories began to surface, and I understood that I had experienced a heart attack. I faintly recalled the ambulance ride and lying in a hospital bed, struggling to open my eyes, while voices floated around me. The thought crossed my mind: could my experience in New Orleans have triggered this?

One morning, as KJ, Keith, Layla, and I shared a meal, a sudden wave of memories crashed over me, much like a sack of oysters falling from a great height. I vividly remembered the ghostly figure of KJ's mother's twin, and that recognition sent waves of anxiety through my chest. Instinctively, I clutched my chest and leaned forward, causing panic to ripple among everyone. Layla's voice cut through the noise, asking if I was okay, but despite my best efforts, I couldn't find the words to reassure her. My mouth moved, but silence prevailed. I could feel her worry escalating as she exclaimed, Dee, what's wrong? Do you need a doctor?

Finally, I managed to shake my head to indicate I was alright. I took a deep breath, wanting to calm her anxieties, and then smiled at her. Despite my effort, I could still see concern etched on her face, so I stood, took a breath, and walked around the table to give her a heartfelt hug. I felt her tension dissipate a little, and I took that moment to retreat to the bedroom to gather my thoughts.

After a few moments, KJ entered and asked if any memories had returned to me. I told him that some fragments had started to resurface, but I was really curious about how he knew so much. With warmth in his voice, he explained that she had shared that I was with her during my time of unconsciousness. He encouraged me to reflect on the past five years we had spent together. I was astonished by the thought that he had been part of our lives for that long. As I pondered his words, he left the room, prompting me to engage in some introspection.

Has it really been five years? It feels like just yesterday that he joined our household. Time has passed swiftly, and yet it feels surreal. What did he mean by saying, I was with her during my unconsciousness? I remembered being in New Orleans, yes, but how did I get there? I recalled that Layla and KJ mentioned something about someone resembling Maymay, which sparked my curiosity about whether she had a twin. So many questions filled my mind. Would I ever fully untangle these thoughts and memories?

Despite the uncertainty, I felt a flicker of excitement at the prospect of understanding it all. I knew that with time and the support of my friends, I would continue to piece together this puzzle, one memory at a time.

Chapter Three

To grasp the reasons behind my recent hospital visit, I decided to take a moment to truly reflect on my life. So, I settled back on my bed, closed my eyes, and let the memories wash over me. Instantly, a vivid picture of my childhood neighborhood came to mind. At the corner stood a charming two-story building; at its base was the Hi Note bar, with its iconic Falstaff beer sign welcoming all who passed.

Right above the bar was a double shotgun house that was home to my dear friends, Keith and Layla, who lived side by side. Next door was another double shotgun, its sturdy cinder block walls telling stories of countless shared moments. My family occupied one side, while the Mcgee's were on the other. Adjacent to us was a delightful single-family home with a long front porch, where Maymay and her family enjoyed warm evenings, inviting the neighborhood to join in on the fun. Their house was unique; unlike the typical shotgun layout, it had rooms sprawling on both sides. Our home, in contrast, featured a straight sightline from the front door to the back, with no twists or turns, just a straight path through our lives.

I also remember when Devell's family filled the space that used to be Sam's grocery store on Lizzardi Street.

Among the sweetest memories from those carefree days was the arrival of the ice cream man. The sound of his truck echoed like a joyful anthem, coaxing us out of our homes. As we spotted him approaching, excitement bubbled over, and we would push and shove, racing to be the first to greet him. Momma, the ice cream man is coming, rang out from every corner. Once we got our treats, we would gather on the porch, relishing every lick of our delicious rewards.

Another favorite activity was playing tag in the massive mulberry tree in my backyard. One person would count while we scrambled to climb its towering branches, which reached over the roofs of nearby homes. In winter, the tree was bare, its strong limbs exposed. But in the summer, it became a leafy fortress where we could leap from house to house, all while trying to avoid being tagged. Reflecting as an adult, I chuckle at how reckless we were; the houses stood just four to five feet apart, and we were just kids chasing laughter.

During those delightful years, Maymay, Keith, and I were truly inseparable. We grew up together, from the crib to kindergarten, and people constantly teased us about who would eventually marry Maymay. Friends believed it was obvious that our connection would lead to a romance, but deep down, I knew that it was Keith who adored her most. Then, when Layla moved into our neighborhood at the age of eight, I felt a spark, there was something special about her, and suddenly the age-old question of love felt resolved. It seemed like the universe had aligned; I had Layla, and Keith had Maymay, and despite our youth, everyone sensed that it was only a matter of time before our friendships blossomed into something even richer.

Just as we were starting to explore our budding feelings, Devell joined our circle, and little did we know, he and Maymay shared an undeniable chemistry. This left Keith feeling uncertain about his place in all of it, and as time passed, it became clear that Maymay felt torn between the two of them.

Keith believed he had the upper hand due to their shared history. Whenever Devell was present, he would lead conversations back to our childhood adventures, attempting to keep Devell at bay. Initially, this tactic seemed effective, but Maymay soon noticed and took it upon herself to bridge the gap, encouraging Devell to feel included by explaining our tales in detail. The more Devell became part of our group, the closer he and Maymay grew, which understandably frustrated Keith. Yet, there was little he or anyone else could do to alter the course of their connections.

This journey is filled with complex emotions and memories, but I'm committed to embracing the lessons learned along the way. Life is a beautiful tapestry woven from growth, friendship, and love, and through this reflection, I feel hopeful and optimistic about what lies ahead. Each experience, no matter how challenging, has opened my heart to the importance of connection and resilience, and I'm excited for whatever comes next,

Layla and I began our journey together when we were just twelve years old, and for our very first date, we decided to go to the movies. I promised to pick her up at one o'clock. As I prepared for the day, a whirlwind of excitement and nerves filled me. I knew this was a big step for our relationship, and I sincerely hoped it would be a positive change.

When I arrived at Layla's house, I was greeted at the porch by her father, waiting for me with an intense expression. As I approached him, he unexpectedly raised his voice. My heart raced, I was just a kid, and I had no idea what was going on. All I could see was the severity of his face, which felt almost surreal. He asked me to step inside the house, and although I considered making a run for it, his presence was so commanding that fear held me in place. So, with a mixture of anxiety and curiosity, I followed him inside.

Once inside, he directed me to sit in a chair, and I couldn't shake the feeling that something was off. As he walked around me, shaking his head and pausing to scrutinize me, I sat frozen, wondering what on earth was happening. His pacing felt like it went on for ages, my imagination running wild with possibilities.

Out of the blue, he grabbed my shoulders from behind and exclaimed, Son, what are you going to do about this? I was utterly confused, my mind racing to catch up with the sudden intensity of the situation. He interrupted my thoughts, his voice rising again,

> If you can do manly things, you can answer my question, Now I'll ask you again: what are you going to do about this situation?

At that moment, I realized I had no clue what he meant. He leaned in, his forehead almost touching mine, and I felt a wave of fear wash over me, tears building in my eyes. Just as I braced for the worst, Layla's mother entered and firmly intervened,

> Leave that boy alone,

I cautiously opened my eyes and was relieved to see that her father had stepped back. Then, quite unexpectedly, he punctuated the tension with laughter, a hearty, joyful sound that felt out of place. I was hesitant to join in, still trembling with fear, but as he continued to chuckle, I felt the weight on my shoulders lighten, and soon I found myself laughing along with him. When Layla emerged from her room, confusion mixed with joy as she took in the sight of us laughing together, struggling to understand what was so amusing.

Despite the stomach aches that came from laughing so hard, the joy momentarily overshadowed my earlier fear. We laughed for what felt like ages, perhaps three to four minutes, before the atmosphere shifted once more. Her father's serious demeanor returned, and he pointed his finger at me,

> Don't make me have to repeat this conversation with you, because believe me, there will be no laughter. Do you hear me, boy?

In that moment, I met his gaze with determination and replied,

> Yes, sir. You won't have to talk to me about it again if I can help it.

I managed a small chuckle, but I quickly understood he was serious. On our way to the movies, Layla turned to me and asked what that conversation was about. I admitted I had no clue, but whatever it was, I planned to steer clear of it.

As time went on, the meaning behind that peculiar conversation became clearer, and it certainly shaped my approach to relationships. Looking back, I realize how pivotal that day was, filled with apprehension that transformed into laughter. And ultimately, I knew I wanted to walk a path that would keep me far away from that intimidating expression. In the end, I found joy in pursuing a loving partnership, where respect and understanding would always reign.

Every time I reflect on that story, I can't help but chuckle, even though I still feel that rush of fear and can vividly picture his face as if he were right there with me. On my wedding day, I had a heartfelt conversation with Layla's father, who shared his own experience from that day. He explained how that discussion had mirrored one he'd had with his father-in-law, echoing in his mind throughout his life. It truly made him reflect on the potential consequences of poor choices and inspired him to grow into a better person. He encouraged me, when the time came for me to have a daughter, to do the same. As he spoke, I found myself thinking that I could never put anyone through that. Yet, when my daughter was born, cradled in my arms, I was reminded of Layla's father's words. In that moment, everything clicked, and I wholeheartedly embraced the idea of sharing those lessons with my little girl.

Layla and I have always known in our hearts that our bond was forever. While Keith and Maymay appeared to be a couple, their relationship felt different from ours. They clearly cared for each other, but there was a certain depth in our connection that theirs hadn't yet reached; it remained in the realm of friendship. Keith tried so hard to get Maymay to commit, but she repeatedly told him she cherished him as a friend and questioned why they couldn't simply enjoy that. That summer, as we turned fifteen, Maymay began dating Devell, and it was heartbreaking to witness Keith's devastation. We continued to hang out as a group, and sometimes Keith would bring a date, which I thought meant he was coping well. However, as time went on, it was evident that the situation was still painful for him. The tension between him and Devell escalated to the point where I often had to step in to diffuse potential fights. Eventually, Keith distanced himself from us, and that was incredibly tough for me. It felt like losing a brother.

In our neighborhood, Keith's family was regarded as well-off. At the start of the school year, he always had new clothes and the latest gear. One Christmas, their tree was brimming with presents, so much so that it looked like a celebration for a family with several children. I still remember one particular holiday when every kid in our circle received bikes with banana seats and foot brakes, while Keith's parents gifted him a stunning twenty-six-inch ten-speed bike. We affectionately named it the Yellow Mobile, as its vibrant canary yellow made it stand out as the fastest bike around. When I first laid eyes on it, it was love at first sight. The first time he let me ride it, I felt as though I were soaring. Whenever we rode through the neighborhood, he confidently led the way. One adventurous day, we decided to take on the notorious Claiborne Bridge. Keith zipped to the top effortlessly, while the rest of us struggled with our one-speed bikes. As he waved from the top, the bridge unexpectedly began to rise. He sped back down, legs pumping furiously, leaving us in awe, as he zoomed past us like we were standing still. We didn't attempt that bridge again until we were much older. It took three years for my parents to finally get me a ten-speed of my own, and while I adored my red bike, it never quite measured up to the Yellow Mobile.

After school, Keith's mom, Mrs. Shirley, always had the most wonderful snacks ready, inviting many kids to hang out at their house. She prepared an assortment of hot sausage po'boy sandwiches cut into bite-sized pieces, perfect for sharing, along with chips and sometimes a delightful fruit salad with mixed fruits and whipped cream. Initially, I hesitated to try that unique combination, but after my first bite, I was utterly hooked; the flavors blended together beautifully,

We were on the basketball team together, and the day we triumphed over the top team in the district was truly unforgettable. Mrs. Shirley greeted us with a delicious gumbo, and after we devoured the meal, she brought out a plate of beignets. It was such an incredible day, one that will forever be etched in my memory.

Keith and his father shared a truly special bond. He once shared with me that every time his father came home, he would immediately look for him, no matter how tired or late he was. Mr. Jackson always found time and energy to play with his son. I loved the image of Keith sometimes waking from a deep sleep to the booming, joyous sound of his father's voice, calling out, Where's my boy? He would leap from his room into his father's embrace, who would whirl him around and toss him lightly into the air, so close to the ceiling, when he caught him, he'd lift him onto his shoulders and proudly tell him how he was turning into a little man. Those moments were filled with love and happiness, creating precious memories that Keith would carry with him.

When Keith was a child, the thought of his father not working really excited him. He spent countless days thinking of all the things him and his father could do if he didn't have to work. They could've gone to City Park, or spend weekends fishing at Lake Pontchartrain, or go to a Saints game, or when he got home from school his father could have been there to help him with his homework. Keith yearned to spend more time with his father, but never having enough time was the predominant reason Mr. Jackson gave him for not being able to do more things with him. Keith thought if his father hadn't worked so hard, he would have been the best father ever.

On the rare occasion when his father had the day off, they went to the barbershop to get their hair cut. At the barbershop, there were other fathers and sons sitting around talking. All the fathers talked about amusing things their sons had done since the last time they were there. Keith didn't know about the other children's fathers, but his father rarely chuckled like that at home. After they were finished at the barbershop, they would go to Ross' Diner on Forstall Street for ice cream. When the waitress came to the table, his father would say,

Little man, what would you like?

Keith would reply the same answer every time,
Two scoops please.

They sat there eating their ice cream, and talking for what seemed like hours. He couldn't remember what they talked about; all he knew was he loved being with his father. Those times were too few and far in between as far as Keith was concerned, and to him those were precious father son moments he never forgot.

One of the things everyone loved about Mr. Jackson was his ability to tell an interesting story. He told a story so well it felt like it was something you had experienced. Sometimes his father told hilarious stories about work that made you laugh weeks later, and other times he told stories that tugged on your emotions. One day his father told a story about his boss Mr. Dilly, Mr. Jackson said he was buffing the hallway as he did every morning when he heard his boss yelling down the hall,

Boy, I need to see you in my office.

Mr. Jackson said he turned around to see who he was speaking to. When his boss saw him look over his shoulder, he became agitated and yelled again,

Boy, I'm talking to you.

It took all of Mr. Jackson's strength not to run down the hall and grab him by the neck to prove he wasn't a boy, but he knew that wasn't an option, so he went into the office. Mr. Jackson stood at the door while Mr. Dilly sat at his desk. His boss pointed to a chair sitting in front of him and asked Mr. Jackson to have a seat. The room was silent for a couple of seconds then Mr. Dilly said,

I've decided not to call the police because I think we can handle this problem ourselves, all you have to do is return the items.

Mr. Jackson sat there confused, not knowing if he should get up and run or find out what was going on. He told him that someone came in during the night and stole a bunch of blank checks, and he was going to get to the bottom of what happened one way or another. The buzz around the office was that a supervisor had been suspended for being on the property after hours, so Mr. Jackson sat there in disbelief, wondering how anyone could accuse him of stealing. Something deep down told him it had to be a joke, but his boss expression assured him the seriousness of the matter. He told him the police would be summoned, and he would lose his job unless the checks were returned. Mr. Jackson said he thought his worst nightmare had come true; he was going to prison. He thought there was nothing he could do or say to clear his name. Just as he began explaining how badly he needed his job, he heard laugher coming from behind him, apparently it was a hoax, but to him it was torture in the worst way. He thought what a sick sense of humor. At the end of this weird story, we children didn't get it and looked at each other in horror. But the old men seemed to understand.

Everyone laughed when Mr. Jackson finished telling the story, but his eyes were tearing. No one else seemed to see through the laughter, but Keith could see his father's pain. He wanted to ask him what was wrong, but he couldn't.

Years later he understood the laughter and tears because he went through the same sort of humiliation.

Hidden Emotions

Chapter Four

M r. Jackson proudly stood as one of the first Black employees at Jax Brewery, recognized as the largest independent brewery in the South and the 10th largest in the entire country. This remarkable achievement was a significant point of pride for him, even though he faced numerous challenges along the way. One of the most pressing issues was his initial inability to join the union, which left him open to layoffs at any moment. While he would typically return from layoffs after just a few weeks, he would come back without any seniority. Fortunately, after years of resilience and persistence, he finally joined the union, feeling a sense of relief that his troubles were behind him.

However, about a month after one of the company's substantial layoffs, a courageous group of Black co-workers banded together to address concerns regarding the fairness of promotions and the layoff process. They highlighted that, despite being union members, Black employees were disproportionately affected by layoffs. Encouraged by his colleagues, they asked Mr. Jackson to join their complaint, but he hesitated, believing he had worked too hard to put his job at risk.

To ensure transparency, Mr. Jackson decided to speak with his boss about the issue, expressing his desire to distance himself from the complaint. He had thrived in his position for twelve years and felt he was treated fairly by the company. In the wake of the complaint, the brewery started hiring new employees while laying off others. Unfortunately, most of those affected were Black. Despite warnings from coworkers and his own suspicions, Mr. Jackson reassured himself that his position was secure, until the day he received the unfortunate news of his layoff. The blow was devastating.

After years of diligent work, Mr. Jackson found himself unemployed and grappling with confusion and disbelief. He had always held the belief that those without jobs simply lacked motivation and shouldn't complain about their circumstances. But now, he found himself in that very situation, and it left him feeling deeply disillusioned with the system that had once seemed so reliable.

In the aftermath of his layoff, Mr. Jackson's spirit changed dramatically. He became withdrawn, spending countless hours in bed or slouched in a recliner, glued to the television.

His wife, Mrs. Shirley, tirelessly encouraged him to reinvigorate his job search, assuring him that he was still a healthy, capable man in a world teeming with opportunities. Yet Mr. Jackson resisted, fearing that the higher-ups could lay him off again at any moment. The humiliation of such an experience was too much to bear, leading him to forgo job hunting altogether. This decision resulted in significant challenges for the family. With Mr. Jackson not working, small comforts like after-school snacks disappeared, forcing their son Keith to sometimes find dinners at friends' homes.

Keith was surprised and saddened by the change in his father's demeanor. All his life, he had craved for his father to be present, but now that he was home, they found it increasingly difficult to connect.

Eventually, Mrs. Shirley could no longer tolerate the complaints and offered a gentle yet firm ultimatum: it was time for Mr. Jackson to either find work or consider moving out, allowing her the chance to thrive. Out of love for his family and a desire to contribute, Mr. Jackson recognized the truth in her words and committed himself to the job search. He dedicated hours to filling out applications and attending interviews, but as time wore on, the process began to feel overwhelming. Recognizing her husband's declining confidence, Mrs. Shirley made a conscious effort to uplift him, ensuring he felt valued and appreciated. However, the disappointment etched on Mr. Jackson's face by the end of his search was hard to miss.

After several months of searching, Mr. Jackson couldn't shake the feeling that others viewed him as one of the "losers" he had previously judged. The more he confronted his circumstances, the more anger emerged, leading him to reckon with the realities of racism that had also impacted his life profoundly.

This situation weighed heavily on the Jackson family. Mrs. Shirley, wishing to protect her husband's pride, requested Keith to refrain from expressing any complaints while his father was at home. They were facing tough times together; their supplies were dwindling, and Keith couldn't recall the last time he received any new clothes or shoes to accommodate his growth spurts. With Mrs. Shirley unable to work, Mr. Jackson's unemployment turned their daily lives into a struggle. He began to believe that perhaps his family would be better off without him, despite their unwavering support, which often felt insufficient in the face of their challenges.

Yet, there remained a flicker of hope, a path forward that could reshape their lives if they emerged from this difficult chapter together, fueled by resilience, love, and a community willing to stand by them.

One day at school, an unexpected incident occurred when Keith fainted, sparking concern and confusion among his peers. He was quickly taken to the nurse's office, where the attentive nurse noticed that Keith was suffering from hunger. She promptly took him to the cafeteria, and that's when I learned about his situation. On our way home, Keith confided in me that he hadn't had a proper meal in two days, with his family surviving solely on bread and butter. My heart sank at his words. I should have picked up on the clues; during lunch, Keith often isolated himself, clearly embarrassed by the food he brought. It was evident that, although he didn't qualify for free lunch, his family's pride prevented them from informing the school about their need for support. However, thanks to Keith's conversation with the nurse, he received a form to take home for his parents to fill out.

When Mr. Jackson saw the form, he was visibly distressed, but ultimately, he recognized that this was a step toward a better situation for their family. As Keith watched his parents fill out the form, he felt their anguish deeply. Mr. Jackson's hands trembled, and Mrs. Shirley sat beside him, her head bowed in sadness. Keith wished he could reassure them that he didn't mind receiving assistance, he wanted to ease their pain, but he feared his words would only complicate matters.

For the first couple of weeks after receiving free lunch, Keith stood in line with his head down, as if he were doing something wrong. I wished I could help him realize that there was no shame in accepting help. Initially, it seemed as though he would eat only half of what he was given, often discarding the rest. I believe he was trying to convey that he didn't truly need the free lunch. But as time passed, a positive change began to emerge. He adjusted to the program and started consuming all of his meal. In fact, it wasn't long before he was happily finishing leftover lunches from friends who couldn't finish theirs, eagerly accepting what was offered.

Life at home, however, was becoming increasingly difficult for Keith's family. One day, they were notified that their telephone service would be disconnected, and this news sent Mr. Jackson into distress. Mrs. Shirley felt an urgent need to tell him, knowing he would ask about job opportunities when he returned home. When she broke the news, Mr. Jackson erupted in anger. Keith noticed that his mother looked frightened as she attempted to calm him down, but her efforts were met with louder shouts. In a moment of heightened tension, Mr. Jackson raised his hand as if to strike her.

No, Daddy,

Keith cried out, his voice filled with fear and desperation.

Mr. Jackson paused when he saw the sadness and fear in Keith's eyes, and in that moment, he seemed to snap back to reality. He looked at his wife, hesitated, and ultimately lowered his hand before storming out of the house. Keith could sense the conflict within his mother; she wished to intervene but knew the potential consequences of doing so. It was a heartbreaking scene that left Keith confused about his father's anger and its effect on their family. His mother tried to explain that it wasn't their fault his father was struggling to find work; it was simply a tough situation that made it hard for a proud man like Mr. Jackson to cope.

Fueled by curiosity, Keith yearned to understand why his father couldn't secure a job and why they were facing such hardships. He sought reassurance, turning to his mother for answers, but she could offer little comfort, trying her best to maintain hope when it was clear she felt uncertain. This was the first time Mr. Jackson had left home, though he was only gone for a couple of days. When he returned, however, he appeared to be in a much better place emotionally. He redoubled his efforts to find work and committed himself to being a good father and husband once again.

Through these challenges, Keith and his family showed resilience and determination. Their journey highlighted the importance of support and understanding in difficult times, proof that even in hardship, there's a path to hope and healing.

One sunny afternoon, Mr. Jackson, Keith, and I found ourselves at the barber shop when our good friend Devell made a surprising entrance. It was as if fate had brought him to us. When we wrapped up at the barbershop, Mr. Jackson suggested we head to the movies, followed by lunch at Ross' Diner. After enjoying a hearty meal, he asked if we'd like to indulge in some ice cream. Keith was absolutely thrilled; he didn't want our perfect day to come to an end. When he got home, he excitedly recounted the day to his mother, but instead of sharing in his joy, she erupted with anger. She demanded to know where his father was, and when Keith explained that his father had taken Devell home, he couldn't understand the reason behind her frustration. To him, it was an unforgettable day spent with his dad, and he felt disheartened that his mother was overshadowing it.

When Mr. Jackson returned home, he was met with a storm of emotions. Before he could even step inside, his wife confronted him, her voice rising in frustration.

> How could you do this to our family? You know we struggle to make ends meet, and you're spending money we can't afford,

Before she could say anything more, he stepped back outside, needing a moment to breathe.

That night, when he came home again, he could sense that everything had shifted. Over time, Keith noticed the weight of frustration in his father's body language, a reflection of the strain that came from not being able to support his family. Simultaneously, Keith saw his mother pulling away, resigned to the reality of their situation. Mrs. Shirley felt trapped in a marriage that was falling apart and could see very clearly that there was little anyone could do to mend it. She encouraged Mr. Jackson to seek help, hoping for a turnaround, but he felt too defeated to comply.

One day, Keith accidentally overheard a conversation between his parents about their future. Mr. Jackson mentioned that leaving might open the way for welfare. Keith's heart sank. He feared that his presence was only prolonging their unhappiness. He heard his mother's tears and sensed a deep sorrow, but he didn't hear her plead for his father to stay. Mrs. Shirley had tried countless ways to bring joy back into their lives, yet fatigue and despair had worn her down, leading her to accept that she would have to let go.

Not long after that tense discussion, Mr. Jackson moved out. While there was a part of Keith that felt a pang of hurt, he ultimately recognized that his father's decision was made with the hope of bettering the family's situation. He watched as his mother spiraled into a deep sadness, and her resentment toward his father grew. Sometimes, she would walk through the house exclaiming,

> He could've put in more effort, I can only guess he's with someone else. How could I have believed he was leaving for us? I should have seen this coming. I was too trusting.

Their separation took a toll on Mrs. Shirley; her vibrant spirit seemed to fade. I observed over the years how bitterness crept into her life, and while I thought Keith might align with her sentiments, it was evident that he held a deeper understanding toward his father.

Years passed after Mr. Jackson's departure, and one day while Keith and I were chatting, we found ourselves reminiscing about the past. When Keith spoke his father's name, a childlike sparkle briefly lit up his face, a look I had not seen for years. It surprised me because I had expected him to harbor resentment for his father's absence. They had endured so much since he left, yet it appeared Keith held a sense of accountability toward his mother for their struggles. He was determined that when he became a father, he would do things differently. He yearned to spend ample time with his future family, ensuring they understood just how much he loved and cherished them.

In reflecting on their experiences, it became clear that some lessons, though born from difficult situations, could ultimately pave the way for a brighter future. Keith's resolve to be a caring and present father was a testament to his growth and optimism. It was a beautiful reminder that even from hardship, love could flourish and reshape the narrative for the next generation.

Chapter Five

S ometimes, Mrs. Shirley would express her feelings about Mr. Jackson's choices, especially regarding his relationships with women. This would often leave Keith feeling a mix of frustration and sadness. Deep down, he was aware that his mother understood the reasons behind his father's departure, and it felt as if she was painting a picture that suggested his dad didn't care about the family. Everyone knew that Mr. Jackson had returned to live with his mother, and Keith believed that leaving was, in many ways, a necessary step for their family's well-being.

One morning, Keith was jolted awake by his mother's raised voice. Thinking his father might be there to visit, he hurried to the kitchen, curiosity pulling him along. To his surprise, he found Mrs. Shirley standing in front of the refrigerator, which was empty, venting her frustrations about his father once again. Overwhelmed by emotion, Keith couldn't hold back anymore.

Why do you keep blaming him?

Hoping to convey his desire for clarity. With a passionate tone, she replied that a man should always be there for his family through both joyful moments and challenges. She pointed out how many families were struggling during these tough economic times and insisted that his father was now acting like those he often criticized: people who cry about their circumstances instead of taking action to improve them.

His mother, feeling overwhelmed, asked Keith to find something else to do and let her have some space. But Keith felt a spark inside him; he was on the verge of making sense of the complex dynamics in their family. He reminded her that it wasn't fair to treat his father like a villain and pleaded with her to help him understand the full picture. She only stared at him not saying a word. After a minute are so he turned and walked away, knowing the outcome wouldn't be good.

Mrs. Shirley had witnessed her husband struggle under life's pressures and was surprised that he would abandon their family in that moment of need. Her emotions were running high, and it seemed she felt pushed to her limits herself. All she wanted was for Mr. Jackson to have had a bit of faith and belief in what their family could overcome together.

In the early days after his father moved out, he would visit Keith daily, but as time passed, those visits became less frequent. Keith couldn't help but feel uneasy about this shift, often attributing it to his mother's intense feelings. She would question his dad's motivations for visiting, as if she hadn't already heard from him, and she would often voice her displeasure about having him around while claiming she needed to focus on getting their life back on track. It only took moments before her frustration would spill over in an emotional outburst, as she felt a heavy burden to ensure their family's survival was secure. Each time his father tried to share his story, Mrs. Shirley would often interrupt, leaving little room for understanding.

One particular day, Mrs. Shirley was very upset with Mr. Jackson. Standing face-to-face with him, her voice thick with emotion, she exclaimed,

> What happened to the partner I once knew? The decisions you've made have deeply impacted our family. It's hard for me to understand why you keep coming around. It feels like you've moved on without us. What do you truly want from this?

In that moment, feeling the weight of each word, Keith sensed the storm of emotions swirling around them. Mr. Jackson stood there momentarily stunned, caught off guard by the sudden burst of emotion. Before he could collect his thoughts, she firmly instructed him to take his child and leave. Looking back on that moment as an adult, Keith realized that his father's visits always centered around him, never just for a casual check-in on his mother. This might explain why she often treated him with such coldness. She seemed to imply that his father was involved with someone else, but Keith knew that the only other house he and his dad ever visited together was Devell's.

As time passed, Keith could sense his father's hesitation whenever he arrived to pick him up. Mr. Jackson would ring the doorbell, standing in anticipation until Keith bounded outside. Eventually, they figured it would be easier to meet in neutral spots, a barber shop here, a diner there. One day, while enjoying a meal with his father, Devell, and me at Ross's Diner, Keith caught sight of his mother approaching. His father, unaware with his back turned, didn't notice her until it was almost too late. When Mr. Jackson finally recognized Mrs. Shirley watching from outside, her hands firmly planted on her hips, he quickly looked down, and when he looked back up, she was gone. Since he hadn't informed her about the day spent together, he knew there would be some difficult conversations ahead. Keith could see the weight of shame in his father's eyes, he glanced at him, silently seeking support and advice on what to say to his mother later, but it was apparent that Mr. Jackson felt equally lost.

Upon returning home, Keith faced Mrs. Shirley, whose disappointment was deep even without a single word spoken. It seemed less about their time together and more about the secrecy of their plan that irked her.

Following the unexpected encounter at the diner, Mr. Jackson decided it was unfair to keep their meetings a secret from Mrs. Shirley. A consensus was reached that he would pick Keith up at home, with complete transparency. This worked for a time, improving their interactions. However, the ongoing tension and arguments that followed during those visits began to take their toll, leading Mr. Jackson to eventually halt those pickups altogether.

On the rare occasions Keith spotted his father in the neighborhood, he was struck by how much older Mr. Jackson seemed to be getting, almost overnight. Once a robust figure with a welcoming smile, his father now appeared weary. His hair, once neatly groomed, frequently lay unkempt, and his beard had outgrown its usual trim. Strands of gray were increasingly taking over the black it used to boast. He often walked with his shoulders hunched, his gaze fixed downward, and he didn't seem to radiate health or vitality anymore. This change deeply concerned Keith, as he sensed a dimming spark in his father's spirit. Occasionally, when Keith would see his dad out on the street, it felt as though Mr. Jackson would deliberately turn away, as if trying to hide the effects of life's burdens from him.

Despite the challenges that lay ahead, Keith held onto the hope that brighter days were possible. His heart swelled with determination to reconnect and support his father. Together, step by step, they could navigate the ups and downs of their lives, reaffirming their bond and lifting each other up in the tough times.

Mr. Jackson may not have had formal education, but he firmly believed in the power of hard work and finding fulfillment in what you do. However, during job interviews, he could feel the judgment from potential employers, and deep down, he knew the outcome. After facing numerous challenges in his job hunt, he took the time to reflect on his life and the choices made along the way. His grandmother shared some wisdom from his father, who realized too late the opportunities that education can bring, better job prospects, security, and more choices in life. It was this understanding that opened his eyes to the reality of being an uneducated Black man in America.

Mr. Jackson also carried the weight of his father's legacy, a man who bravely sought to start a union in the 1930s despite the tremendous risks involved, and tragically paid the ultimate price. He still vividly remembers that painful chapter from his childhood, witnessing the heartbreaking scene of his father's sacrifice in their small country yard.

When Mr. Jackson was about twelve years old, he and his mother sat down to talk about what happened to his father. She was surprised that not only did he remember what happened, but recalled what was said to them as they watched. The men said,

This is what happens to trouble maker niggers.

His mother remembered him squeezing her leg as they set her husband's body on fire. They forced the whole family to watch, all the while warning that they could be next.

When Mr. Jackson and his mother were having their talk, he apparently made a conscious decision not to put his family through what they had endured. His philosophy on life was a direct result of that night. Mr. Jackson understood why his dad did what he did, even though he knew it would cost him his life.

Once Mr. Jackson embraced his past, he decided to take a bold step by enrolling in night school. He was filled with hope that these classes would pave the way for a new and rewarding career through a training program. Reflecting on his life, he wished he had stood up against the system like his father instead of succumbing to it. He came to the realization that accepting injustice didn't protect his job; it ultimately led to the loss of both his employment and his family. The anger he felt often clouded his ability to focus on his studies. Unfortunately, when Mr. Jackson made the tough choice to drop out of the program, he came to understand that he had waited too long for change.

On a warm summer evening, Mrs. Shirley received a heart-wrenching call from her mother-in-law, sharing the devastating news that Mr. Jackson had passed away. At that moment, Keith was in his room. He was jolted by a terrible yell followed by a thump. Rushing out, he found his mother on the floor, with the phone lying beside her. Unsure whether to grab the phone or attend to her, he gently supported her head and began to speak in soothing tones.

Mom, are you okay? Can you hear me?

When Mrs. Shirley remained unresponsive, panic surged through him, and he called out, once again. Slowly, she began to regain her senses, and Keith heard a voice on the phone. He hesitated to answer, sensing the news would not be good. He listened in silence until his worst fears were confirmed:

Your father is gone.

His immediate instinct was to ask, Gone where? But deep down, he understood the meaning. He laid the phone down, striving to remain strong for his mother as tears streamed down his cheeks. Looking at her, he gained a new perspective. It became clear that she deeply loved his father, and her previous frustration stemmed from the overwhelming situation he had found himself in, not from any resentment towards him.

The funeral was a touching celebration of Mr. Jackson's life. Friends from his past gathered to share fond memories and recall the laughter he brought with him to the barber shop. They remembered his great stories, and there was a warmth in the reminiscing, a reminder of the vibrant spirit he had been. Conversations turned to the pain he experienced when he felt unable to care for his family, an acknowledgment of the battles he faced.

While the exact cause of his passing remained unclear, many felt he had essentially succumbed to a broken heart. His concealed emotions prevented him from confronting the changes in his life. He couldn't envision that one day, things could improve and that sometimes enduring the storms of life leads to brighter days. In his heart, Mr. Jackson saw himself as a failure, and no one could convince him otherwise that his journey wasn't over.

Chapter Six

W hen Layla and I stepped into George Washington Carver High School, we were already a strong couple, just like Devell and Maymay. Our favorite date nights revolved around exhilarating football games where Devell shone as both quarterback and leader. After each game, we would head to K&B Drugstore, famous for serving the most delicious hamburgers and crispy french fries that kept us coming back for more.

Keith had experienced a few relationships, but none had developed into anything serious. Then, in a delightful twist during our mid-senior year, Devell surprised everyone by proposing to Maymay, and she joyfully accepted. I noticed a flicker of disappointment in Keith, but he remained remarkably composed. After high school, Devell enlisted in the Air Force, and before long, the wedding was called off.

Yet, life has its surprises. Keith and Maymay reconnected, and in no time, they became a couple themselves. Many people envisioned a future with the four of us as couples, creating shared experiences and memories. Layla and I tied the knot two years after graduation, and Keith and Maymay followed suit just a year later. It was a time filled with joy as we celebrated each other's milestones. When Devell completed his service, I could sense Keith's anxiety about his past with Maymay, but he soon realized he had nothing to fear.

A truly unforgettable moment in my life was when Layla gave birth to our beautiful daughter. It brought us even closer than I ever thought possible. We were thrilled to have Keith and Maymay as our daughter's godparents, and it lit up their faces with joy. Still, it was clear that deep down, they wished for a child of their own one day.

In the blissful early days of their marriage, every time Maymay experienced a slight delay in her period, even for just a day, she and Keith would dream up plans for their future children. They would chat excitedly about what sports their child might play or which college he might attend. Sadly, their hopes would come crashing down whenever she received her period. After years of yearning, they came to terms with their journey regarding parenthood, embracing a new narrative.

Maymay stood five feet five inches tall and weighed around one hundred ten pounds, always maintaining a polished appearance. Both girls ensured they visited the salon every two weeks for hair and nails, always looking fabulous. One day, Maymay found herself in a bit of a predicament when she suddenly remembered a party she and Keith were invited to the very next day. Rushing to the salon for an emergency appointment, she learned that her regular stylist was unavailable. In her moment of need, she reluctantly decided to go with Evelynn, a stylist renowned for her edgy creativity. Although many clients adored her unique styles, Maymay hesitated. Still, trusting Evelynn's promise to keep her look conservative, she moved forward.

After the appointment, Maymay gazed into the mirror, and to her horror, it felt as if she had half of her hair shaved off. Layla quickly sensed her distress and tried to reassure her that it looked nice, but it was clear that Maymay was quite upset. In a moment of frustration, she confronted Evelynn and left without paying. However, after a few days, she returned to settle the bill, having grown fond of her new hairstyle. From that day forward, Evelynn became her go-to stylist, and Maymay couldn't have been happier with the results.

Just a few weeks after the party, Maymay fell ill. Concerned, Layla took her to Charity Hospital since she wasn't showing any signs of improvement. By this time, Maymay found it tough to even get out of bed and was unable to keep food down. The doctor provided medication and sent her home, and Layla devoted herself to nursing her back to health. As Maymay's weight began to dwindle, Layla made the wise decision to return to the hospital. She explained all the troubling symptoms to the doctor, who finally suggested that Maymay could possibly be pregnant. Those words felt like music to Maymay's ears, as she had longed to hear such news for years. But she remained cautious, determined to stay calm until confirmation, especially considering her past experiences with false pregnancies. This time felt different; she had never felt so unwell before. Maymay decided to keep the news from Keith until the test results came through, even though the thought of keeping such a secret was tough, because of the dreams they had of parenthood.

One night, as she slept, Keith suddenly woke her up with a question,

What do you mean you're pregnant?

Bewildered, Maymay realized she must have been talking in her sleep. With a smile, she playfully pretended not to know what he meant and encouraged him to go back to sleep, her heart racing with excitement at the possibilities ahead.

I'll never forget the moment Maymay got that life-changing call from the doctor. When he delivered the incredible news that she was expecting, her face lit up like a bright star. She was so overwhelmed with joy that she yelled,

Layla, we did it. We did it,

Then started running around the room in pure excitement. Layla had to gently grab her and remind her to take a breath, warning that if she didn't calm down, she might end up hurting herself in her enthusiasm. Maymay was just bursting at the seams with happiness; she couldn't even wait for Keith to come home to share her amazing news.

When Keith finally arrived and she told him, I was taken aback by his response, he just stood there with a blank expression for a moment. Then, he broke into an exuberant declaration, shouting that he was the biggest and strongest man alive. Now, mind you, he's about five foot ten and weighs around 170 pounds, always looking sharp with that neat haircut and well-groomed goatee. It's so entertaining that he sees himself as a powerhouse, especially since I've seen him struggle with a 140-pound bench press,

One day at the gym, he decided to challenge himself with a 150-pound snatch lift. He managed to lift it triumphantly over his head, looking so proud. But suddenly, his legs started shaking, and I could see the panic setting in on his face. Acting quickly, I rushed in to help by placing the weights down beside him, even though he insisted he didn't need a hand and had everything under control. As we walked out together, he quietly said, "Thank you," and I nodded with a smile as we carried on with our day. His idea of being the biggest and strongest felt a little exaggerated, especially given his struggles with the weights.

The day after Maymay's big news, Keith couldn't contain his excitement. He bolted around the neighborhood in shorts and bare feet, despite the chilly 40-degree weather, shouting,

I'm going to be a father. I, Keith, am gonna be a father,

Layla and I exchanged bewildered glances, I genuinely thought he was losing it. And then, out of nowhere, Layla grabbed a coat and ran outside, which surprised me since she's never been keen on the cold. I recalled our wedding day, which was a brisk fifty degrees, and how she almost considered canceling everything just to avoid the chill.

Whenever we talked about the cold, she would recount a childhood story that always made me chuckle. She remembered being in New York City with her mother, waiting for a bus to visit Aunt Edith when a fierce wind swept in, making it freezing. The buses were late due to snow, and she complained that her tears froze on her cheeks. That experience made her swear off visiting cold places in winter.

So, seeing her race outside without a coat on one of the coldest days of the year was a shock. I heard her telling Keith he would be a "dead father" if he didn't dress warmly. He seemed completely oblivious as he jumped around, still whooping with joy. I had expected her to chase him down, but instead, she dashed back inside, handed me my coat and shoes, and urged me to go cover Keith up. I grabbed them quickly and bolted outside.

The instant I stepped out, the brisk air hit me like a wall. I glanced up to see Keith a block away, still in his shorts, so I took a deep breath and sprinted toward him. The closer I got, the faster he seemed to run. There were times I thought about stopping, especially when a bus splashed icy water all over me, or when a car slid dangerously close behind me. But nothing could dampen the exhilarating sense of joy and anticipation that filled the air. What a beautiful time for all of us.

My heart raced with excitement and adrenaline after that intense chase. As I dashed around, determined to catch up, I spotted him turning yet another corner. The effort was starting to wear on me, and I couldn't shake the thought of whether I'd actually be able to catch him. I knew that reaching the next corner was crucial, so I pushed myself even harder. Just as I rounded the bend, I was met with a surprising sight: police officers had surrounded him. As soon as the officers caught sight of me sprinting around the corner, they drew their guns, and I instantly halted, perhaps a bit too abruptly for my own good. The coat flew one way, the shoes another, and down I went. Before I knew it, an officer was standing over me, his foot resting firmly in the center of my back.

Meanwhile, Keith was gasping for air, struggling to convey to the officers that he hadn't done anything wrong, he was just excitedly celebrating his wife's pregnancy. I quickly gathered my breath and started to explain the situation. Keith was doubled over, hands on his knees, frantically trying to regain his composure. The officers loomed over me; their guns still aimed in my direction. Finally, as he caught his breath, Keith shouted out that everything was fine, beginning to explain what had happened. They looked at us as though we had completely lost our mind. I couldn't help but chime in,

It's true. He's going to be a dad.

With that, Keith shared how long he and his wife had been trying for this baby and how it had finally come to fruition. In a wave of excitement, Keith started jumping up and down, shouting,

I'm going to be a father. I'm going to be the best father there ever was.

The officers, taken aback by his enthusiasm, shifted their attention from me to him.

"Sir, please," I said quickly, "he's just really happy.

After a moment of confusion and apprehension, one of the officers reminded us to be a bit more mindful in our celebrations, as they could lead to serious consequences. I couldn't help but think how strange it was that joy could be perceived this way, but I decided it was better to hold my tongue, after all, no one really appreciates it when you mouth off during a tense situation.

After a while, the officers wrapped up their conversation and left. I quickly collected the scattered belongings and tossed them over to Keith, playfully asking if he had completely lost his mind since we could've ended up in serious danger. As we started walking back home, I noticed Keith donned my shoes and had thrown my coat around his shoulders. Surprisingly, while he was sweating from all the excitement, I felt like ice. Breathing felt like a challenge, with pressure sitting heavily on my chest. I stopped, bent over, and grasped my knees for support. Keith noticed and kindly handed me the coat, saying,

Looks like you need this more than I do.

Unfortunately, the next week found me in bed, battling a fever and feeling utterly miserable. The first two days were especially tough; my appetite vanished completely. Layla found the situation amusing, teasing me about whether I was sure I wasn't pregnant myself. As Keith proudly paraded around proclaiming his new father status, there I was, lying in bed, fighting off illness, while Layla insisted, I just had a cold.

After spending days in bed, fighting through the discomfort, I started to feel an unsuspected paranoia creeping in. It's incredible how our minds can play tricks on us when we're under the weather. I half-convinced myself that Keith was deliberately keeping me from meeting his new baby, which upset me deeply. Why hadn't he stopped by to check on me? My mind spun with conspiracy theories, attributing his absence to some sort of plot to push me out of the picture. But as I began to recover, it became clear that he was simply caught up in the joy of his growing family.

Throughout the pregnancy, Keith and his wife transformed into two buzzing little lovebirds. Whenever you saw them together, they were constantly embracing, stealing kisses, or just enjoying playful moments. Keith would often rub her baby bump and talk to it as if waiting for a response. It was such a heartwarming sight, seeing their happiness really brightened my spirits as I turned the corner on my own recovery.

When Maymay first discovered she was pregnant, her excitement burst forth in the form of adorable maternity clothes. At that stage, she looked as radiant as ever, and while her baby bump wasn't visible just yet, we could sense her eagerness to share this life-changing news with the world. One standout outfit featured charming zippers that ran across her belly, boldly proclaiming, Look out world, I'm on my way. As her pregnancy progressed, she would unzip the pouch to unveil another delightful message: Look out for change because I'm coming. By the time she reached her ninth month, her outfit sported playful eyes peeking out along with the cheerful announcement, I'm here. It was absolutely heartwarming to see her spirit radiate through those outfits.

Keith also joined in on the fun with his collection of unique shirts that added humor to the journey. At first, it was a bit unexpected to see him strutting around in such cheeky attire, but soon everyone embraced his playful approach to fatherhood. One of his funniest shirts depicted a husband telling his wife that he lost the baby, and on the back, a wide-smiling baby cheekily replied, Daddy, I'm back here. It was all in good fun, and you could tell how much joy it brought him to be part of this adventure.

Every time I spotted Maymay, Keith was right there with her, supportive and enthusiastic. He took on household chores with a newfound dedication, whipping up delicious meals and even tackling grocery shopping. In fact, he became so involved that he started to gain a little weight, almost looking like he was expecting alongside Maymay. The more her belly grew, the more joyful he seemed, proudly walking around with a wave of happiness. While some might have found it amusing, it filled my heart to see him so content. They even threw an unforgettable party halfway through the pregnancy that was simply phenomenal.

As the week leading up to the party unfolded, anticipation filled the air. We meticulously planned out the space, dividing the house into three vibrant sections: a fun-filled area for kids, a lively sports zone, and a dance floor where everyone could cut loose. Maymay went all out, she ordered an exciting bounce house and hired a clown who would not only entertain but also look after the little ones. For sports enthusiasts, she rented the biggest TV available, and we prepped for a fantastic live band to create the perfect ambience for dancing.

Although the festivities officially kicked off at noon, we strolled in fashionably late at around two-thirty, thanks to Layla's impressive sense of style. As we stepped into the kitchen, we were greeted by an overwhelming wave of mouthwatering aromas wafting from a delightful spread of food. The counters were a feast for the eyes, featuring everything from sizzling hot dogs, juicy burgers, and delightful sandwiches to finger-licking ribs, spicy hot links, and a generous selection of pasta salads. There was even a crawfish boil area, topped off with a bubbling pot of gumbo that was simply divine. Keith shared that Maymay had been up since four that morning, pouring her heart into preparing each dish. She truly had a gift for cooking, and every Sunday, her home would fill with warm laughter and joyful chatter as friends gathered for her fantastic meals. Walking into that party felt like stepping into a celebration of community and love, and you could see the delight in everyone's eyes as they arrived, the air thick with happiness and anticipation.

The band, aptly named Consensus, was in perfect harmony that day, and music flowed through the air, inviting everyone to dance. They usually played at our neighborhood events, but this time, they sounded absolutely incredible. As the energy escalated, the indoor space filled up, and soon people spilled out into the street, capturing the true spirit of joy and celebration.

Much to our surprise, the police showed up and blocked off the street. Initially, we worried they might disrupt our fun, but happily, they were there to ensure the festivities went as smoothly as possible. By midnight, the party was still in full swing, and guests continued to arrive, eager to share in Maymay and Keith's excitement about becoming parents.

People traveled from every corner of the city to join this remarkable occasion. Originally slated to wrap up at two o'clock in the morning, the celebration was still going strong well beyond three. By five o'clock, we had to weave our way through the crowd to leave, and we later heard the festivities carried on until noon the next day. The band members shared that they didn't leave until around seven o'clock in the morning, remarkable, considering there were still exuberant dancers spreading joy. Keith clearly embraced the celebratory vibe a little too much and was spotted playfully running around with a towel pinned like a cape, joyfully proclaiming himself Superman. Maymay later swooped in to save him from his antics, but then he donned a Batman mask as a fun twist. It was evident that she wanted him to enjoy the moment, recognizing how special this time was for both of them.

While the exact moment the party came to a close remains a delightful mystery, what everyone can agree on is that it was an unforgettable celebration for Maymay, Keith, and the whole neighborhood. The buzz of excitement lingered for weeks, and it seemed that every person I encountered had a cherished memory from that incredible night.

Hidden Emotions

Chapter Seven

The day before KJ's arrival, Maymay had a unique and unsettling intuition that something wasn't quite right. All night, she felt a rhythmic pulsation in her pelvic area that left her uneasy. Once Keith left for work, she reached out to Layla to share her worries. Over the phone, her distress was intense, her voice quivered, and the moans intertwined with her words revealed her anxiety. Convinced she was losing the baby, she urgently asked Layla if we could take her to the hospital.

When Layla and I arrived at her home, we found Maymay doubled over in her kitchen, clutching her stomach, with water pooling around her feet. She breathlessly told us that her water had broken right after she hung up the phone. As we rushed to her side, her cries echoed through the room:

Oh no, I'm losing my baby, please, God, don't let this happen,

Tears streamed down her face as she looked to us for comfort. With a reassuring tone, Layla reminded her,

You're not losing your baby; you're having the baby,

The moment she heard those words, Maymay's expression transformed, the tension in her face easing just a little. Layla swiftly moved to grab the bags that had been meticulously packed ever since they discovered she was pregnant.

Before we set off for the hospital, I called Keith to let him know we were on our way and that Maymay was okay. His reaction was immediate and filled with panic.

It's too early, it's not time, she can't be having the baby, The doctor said it wouldn't be for another two weeks,

I did my best to explain that babies often have their own timelines, and it's impossible to predict their arrival. Through the phone, I could hear his escalating concern. I told him to meet us at Charity Hospital. As I hung up, I caught the tail end of his shouting, but there was no time to respond; we needed to leave.

While driving, my focus was challenged by the heart, wrenching sounds coming from the back seat. After a few minutes, I felt nauseous, and the cacophony made it feel like

I was driving through a chaotic scene. Picture trying to drive amidst the sound of someone being murdered in your back seat, it was overwhelming. I turned to Layla, hoping she could help quiet Maymay down, as the noise was testing my nerves. She urged me to concentrate on the road so we could reach the hospital safely. I took a deep breath and tried to focus on something positive. Gripping the steering wheel, I envisioned our little girl, which brought me a sense of calm, until another agonizing cry from Maymay jolted me back to reality. By the time we arrived at the hospital, I felt disoriented. Maymay, too, looked visibly worn out from the ordeal, and I couldn't shake the feeling that I was experiencing the weight of the moment right alongside her; my stomach was twisted in knots, and I questioned whether I might need medical attention myself.

Thanks to a call we made to her doctor before leaving, she was ready for us upon our arrival. My legs trembled as we walked in, the anxiety almost too much to bear. They quickly placed Maymay in a wheelchair and whisked her away to a room. I felt like I could use a wheelchair myself. I staggered to a chair, momentarily lightheaded and drenched in sweat.

A nurse approached me and asked if I had driven a pregnant woman to the hospital. The sudden question jolted me upright, and I worried something might be wrong with Maymay. But she placed her hand gently on my shoulder, calming me. Don't worry, she said with a warm smile, I recognize the look of a man who's just navigated through the symphony of a pregnant woman's emotions. With a reassuring pat on my shoulder, she added, good man.

As she walked away, a sense of pride swelled within me. Yeah, I am a good man, I thought, ready to support Maymay through this incredible and transformative moment in our lives.

As the nurse carefully wheeled Maymay away, her voice echoed down the hall, calling out in both urgency and strength. It was hard to tell just how far she was moving from us, as her cries seemed to resonate throughout the lobby, growing louder with each passing moment. We sat, filled with anticipation and concern, waiting for Keith to burst through those doors, hoping for good news. After about half an hour, realizing he hadn't come, we decided to make our way to Maymay's room to lend her some comfort.

As we walked down the corridor, we were taken aback by how far away she seemed; her cries made it feel as though she were just around the corner. Every step quickened our pulse as we pushed the door open and heard her cry out for help. The urgency in her voice was clear. Maymay was calling for her doctor, as the arrival of her baby was imminent. Layla, sensing the intensity of the moment, stepped in close and took her hand, trying to soothe her. For a brief moment, Maymay seemed to calm down, but then her voice erupted with renewed strength. It startled Layla, who exclaimed in surprise as Maymay gripped her hand with unexpected power. The sound of their voices blended into a high, pitched symphony of emotion, almost overwhelming in its intensity.

Feeling the urgency of the situation, I dashed out to find a nurse, just as I spotted Keith galloping down the hall. Quickly, I led him to the delivery room. The moment Maymay saw him, a wave of tranquility washed over her face. Her tension seemed to dissipate with his presence; she released Layla's hand and reached out to Keith, who settled in beside her, a reassuring pillar of support.

Layla and I retreated back to the lobby, where the gravity of the situation seemed to lighten. Layla then noticed a strange swelling in her fingers. Given our setting, she sought out a nurse for a quick check-up, which revealed the surprising news that she had two broken fingers. I couldn't help but chuckle every time I looked at the cast on her hand. Eventually, however, Layla lost her sense of humor about it and asked what I found so amusing. With a grin, I confessed that it reminded me of the time she had delivered our daughter. I recalled how she squeezed my hand so tightly that it felt like her grip could shatter my arm all the way up to my elbow.

After hours of waiting in the lobby without any updates, we finally learned from a nurse that Maymay might take another day to deliver. With a mix of hope and exhaustion, we decided it was best to head home, broken hand and all.

The following morning was filled with infectious energy as we awoke to Keith energetically running around the neighborhood, proclaiming that he could take on the world heavyweight champion. His excitement was palpable, though I found it amusing to playfully think about how I could easily overpower him with just one punch, But I chose to let him revel in his joyful moment, as it was one everyone around him cherished.

The neighborhood buzzed with excitement for Maymay and Keith. Whenever she crossed paths with the local women, they began sharing their own memorable stories of childbirth, glorious and grueling in equal measure. Stella, her neighbor, recounted how after giving birth to her twins, she vowed never to do it again. Yet here she was now, happily embracing her four children as if each was a precious gift. My heart swelled with joy for Maymay and Keith; having experienced the bliss of parenthood myself, I understood all too well the incredible feelings they were about to discover. Bringing our daughter into the world had been one of the most profound experiences of my life, and now it was their turn to relish in that extraordinary joy.

When Keith Jr., affectionately nicknamed KJ, finally made his entrance into the world, he weighed five pounds, six ounces and measured about twenty inches long, his delicate skin peeling and ashy. Keith looked on with concern, feeling that KJ, with his fragile appearance, was a far cry from his own robust birth weight of nine pounds, six ounces. The doctor reassured Keith that KJ was perfectly healthy, but doubts lingered in his mind.

At Mrs. Shirley's house, pride radiated from the walls, adorned with pictures of a young Keith, including that cherished first picture the day he returned home from the hospital. His little crooked smile shone brightly, with rosy, chunky cheeks that made every parent's heart swell. Keith wore that picture like a badge of honor, determined for his son to resemble him. He was relentless in his quest to fatten KJ up, returning home during lunch breaks just to feed him. Every day, he weighed KJ, eager to see any signs of growth. It wasn't until KJ hit ten pounds at around two months old that Keith finally relaxed, basking in the happiness that came with being a new father. For those early days, the joy radiated from him, filling our lives with hope and laughter.

KJ was just around a year old when Keith's behavior took a noticeable shift. He began leaving work early quite frequently, confidently insisting that his boss understood his need to be home with his son. It seemed like he believed Maymay couldn't manage everything without him. Initially, she found his protective instincts endearing, but as the surprise visits home became more frequent, a sense of concern began to creep in. There were days when Keith would leave for work only to return within an hour. Maymay started to worry about the ramifications this could have on his job, especially given the economic climate, where jobs were scarce, and unemployment was a significant concern. At that moment, for every person with a job, there were scores of others vying for employment in the same field.

Maymay approached Keith to discuss her concerns, but he seemed unaware of the precarious position he was putting himself in. He remained steadfast in his belief that his boss was supportive of his situation and encouraged her not to worry about job security. When Keith was at home, he would excitedly talk about adventures like going to ballgames, fishing, and creating lasting memories with KJ, experiences he yearned to share after missing out on similar moments with his own father. He was determined not to deny KJ those precious memories. However, Maymay pointed out that to finance those outings, he needed to maintain his job. She frequently inquired about his plans for paying for such activities.

She wanted to convey that being a good father doesn't mean neglecting responsibilities; it's all part of life's intricate dance, and working is essential for survival. At least one of them needed a steady income. Unfortunately, it seemed as though Keith struggled to grasp this reality. His thoughts constantly drifted to KJ when he was at work, his first words, first steps, and his future in school occupied his mind. These reflections began to impact his performance, as he believed work was interrupting his relationship with his son, and he couldn't bear to feel that way. Keith often thought that had his own father been more attuned to emotions, he would have understood what he was going through, perhaps even preventing some of the heartaches Keith had experienced.

One morning, when Keith was just two minutes late for work, he overheard his boss, Bob, chatting with colleagues in the hallway. Bob raised concerns about how Keith was managing his workload, which frustrated him deeply. Keith felt that Bob, who also had a family, should have a better understanding of the joys and challenges that come with being a new father. After all, Bob was often seen taking time off to be with his family. Keith remembered a particular day when he had been looking to hand Bob a completed project due for a customer, only to find that Bob had taken that day off to take his daughter to Audubon Park. Keith couldn't help but feel a surge of anger; it felt completely unjust for Bob to question his dedication to his job when he often prioritized family time.

What stung most was the memory of all the weekends Keith had sacrificed to meet the so, called urgent projects Bob assigned him before KJ's arrival. It felt as though his boss was seeking any reason to fire him. A few weeks later, in the aftermath of a troubling encounter at work, Keith decided to resign.

One bright morning while driving to work, Keith soaked in the gorgeous day, the sun beaming brightly overhead and fluffy clouds lazily drifting by. As he drove, he found himself lost in thought, imagining faces in the clouds, a delightful pastime he had enjoyed since childhood. To his surprise, he spotted a face that strikingly resembled his father, a vision that startled him with its clarity. Glancing in the rearview mirror, he noticed a police car trailing him. Automatically, he checked his speed and felt relieved to see he was within the limit. Still, the uncertainty lingered, had he accidentally run a stop sign or a red light? He couldn't be sure, but he knew his concentration had waned.

Looking back in the mirror, he noticed that the police car didn't have its lights flashing. He continued driving while keeping a watchful eye on both the road and the mirror, his thoughts whirling with anxiety. Questions raced through his mind: Did he have his driver's license? Was the registration in the car? Where was the insurance card? What would he do if he got pulled over? But as his mind began to settle, he reassured himself that they probably weren't following him; they were just on patrol and likely hadn't even noticed him. He chuckled at the absurdity of how an adult could feel such a rush of nervousness over a police vehicle.

As he drove on, the thought of the police faded from his mind, replaced by a captivating view of the sky. To his astonishment, he noticed a figure that resembled his father amidst the clouds. It took everything in him not to slam on the brakes at that moment. Soon, other familiar faces began to emerge, his mother, grandparents, and beloved friends joined his father in the ethereal display. It was such a striking sight; unlike anything he had ever experienced before; it felt as if they were trying to convey an important message to him. Perhaps his father was signaling that he should heed caution and return home for safety. A shiver ran through him, but he resolved to keep his thoughts positive.

A few miles down the road, he glanced in the rearview mirror and saw the police still trailing behind him. Feeling a rush of nerves, he made a few turns to test if they would follow, and indeed, they did. Initially, fear gripped him, but then clarity set in. After all, the police were there to serve and protect the community, and that was something he could find comfort in.

As he neared his workplace, with a mix of hesitation and anticipation, he pulled into the parking lot, momentarily frozen as he considered what might happen next. He glanced up toward the sky in search of his father's face, hoping it might still be there. He scanned the clouds intently, but they were beginning to fade, and the reassuring image was gone. He shifted his focus back to the police, only to realize they hadn't followed him into the parking lot. A wave of relief washed over him.

Just as he prepared to step out of the car, he spotted the officers parked on the street. He decided to wait, curious about what might happen next, would they approach him?

After a brief pause, he opened the car door, intentionally keeping his back to the officers to mask the anxious flicker that must have shown on his face. He walked purposefully toward the entryway. When the officers noticed him exiting the vehicle, they quickly pulled in, jumping out of their car and pointing their guns at him. In that heartbeat, he felt his life flash before his eyes, and shockingly, it brought forth a flood of humor from a cherished childhood memory. Without thinking, he chuckled softly, almost laughing out loud, blissfully lost in the memory.

One day we were walking home from the store when we heard some officers running behind us yelling, Get on the ground, on the ground. We were about thirteen or fourteen, and it scared the crap out of us. We both lay on the ground and stretched our arms out in front of us like we saw on television. As we lay there, the officers went running by, apparently, they were chasing someone else. We were so afraid it took us about several seconds to get up. When we did, we noticed people in the neighboring stores were laughing. At first, we didn't think it was humorous, but the more they laughed the funnier it became. So, when that incident crossed Keith's mind he couldn't control himself, he began laughing. That must have enraged the officers because they were yelling for him to get on the ground. He knew the mentality of the New Orleans Police Department, so he slowly lay down. One of the officers walked over, and kicked him in the ribs, and asked him what was so funny. He couldn't believe what was happening to him; in all his life, he had never been abused by police. He knew it existed but had never experienced it. He tried to think of what laws he had broken, but none came to mind. He asked the officers what was the problem, why were they after him. The more he talked the more agitated the officers became. They were yelling at him to shut up. While he was on the ground, his boss, Bob walked by and stared at him. Keith noticed that Bob seemed to be scared and wondered what he was afraid of because he wasn't the one getting his ass kicked. He looked at Bob again and swore he saw a smile on his face. They placed hand cuffs on Keith, snatched him up, and threw him against the police car. They slammed his face on the hood of the car splitting his lip almost in half while saying things like,

> how long did you think it would take us to find you? Did you have fun while you were out? You can kiss this freedom good bye. You'll be lucky if you don't get the death penalty this time.

Keith tried to tell them they had the wrong guy, but they ignored him. While Keith's body was pressed against the police car with blood dripping from his mouth, Bob walked over to the officer and asked what was the problem. That really aggravated Keith because Bob assumed he was guilty of something. One of the officers said he fit the description of a murderer who escaped from prison.

Keith's eyes almost popped out of his head. Bob asked the officers when did the escape occur. He stared at his boss in disbelief; he wondered what he was trying to prove. Bob knew it was impossible for him to be an escaped convict. He assumed his boss was making fun of him. The officer replied, two days ago. Bob told them they had the wrong guy because Keith had been employed by him for years. Apparently, they didn't believe him because they took Keith to the station anyway.

When he got there, all the officers were staring and taunting him. Whoever they were looking for, must have looked a lot like him. They put Keith into a little room that felt like a cage. He sat there wondering what would happen to his family if something happened to him.

The police officers entered the room and took a seat across the table from Keith, tension hanging in the air. When he inquired about why he was there, silence enveloped the space, no words, just penetrating stares that left him feeling uneasy. They engaged in a classic good cop, bad cop routine: one flashed a friendly smile and offered him a cup of coffee, while the other bore a scowl that suggested he had just stepped on a nail. Then, unexpectedly, a knock interrupted the atmosphere, prompting one officer to excuse himself, leaving just the stern one, who continued to level his unwavering gaze at Keith.

After enduring an exhausting eight hours of silence, he was finally released. Keith was left grappling with a whirlwind of emotions. Was it anger over being detained without cause, or relief that he was free? The mystery deepened later that month when news broke about the capture of a notorious escaped murderer, someone a foot shorter than Keith but with a substantial weight advantage. The absurdity of the contrast often elicits laughter when Keith shares his story; while he too sees the humor in it, it also echoes troubling memories. It reminded him of the painful anecdotes shared by his father clarifying the tears he had once misunderstood.

When Keith made the difficult decision to quit his job, Maymay's reaction was fiery.

> Are you out of your mind? Now what are we going to do? How will we manage our bills?

Her questions came rushing forth, fueled by concern and confusion. The more she pressed, the further he retreated into himself, struggling to articulate why he would leave a steady job without a backup plan. To Maymay, his actions were baffling, especially when others speculated, he was taking a leap into entrepreneurship, a notion he had frequently entertained. Realizing that something needed to be said, I approached him, only to be met with a terse dismissal when he snapped, It's not your business; back off.

Frustrated by constant interference, Keith began to distance himself, finding solace in his home. During one of my visits, I found him in Maymay's old rocking chair, cradling a sleeping KJ. She suggested putting the baby down for a nap, but Keith was adamant, wanting to be the first-person KJ saw when he woke. Maymay shared that each morning, he would scoop up KJ, holding him lovingly until he stirred awake. However, one morning, when Keith spotted Maymay holding KJ, he reacted strongly, snatching the baby away as he retreated to the living room, apologizing profusely for his oversleeping. His intense response raised concerns; it felt excessive and troubling.

During my visit, I encouraged him to reflect on his situation, but he replied with determination, I'm doing this for my son. He wished to foster an unbreakable bond with KJ, yet his fixation on quantity over quality was disconcerting. I reminded him that being a devoted father encompasses far more than physical presence; it's about emotional support, stability, and making responsible choices. Unfortunately, he couldn't see that, convinced that his mere presence equated to fatherhood.

In his mind, if only his father had dedicated more time to the family, perhaps he would still be alive. This connection to his past haunted him, creating an obsession with shaping a better future for KJ. I found it puzzling that someone so seemingly grounded could harbor such strong emotions about his upbringing. Still, it shed light on our earlier conversations. He yearned for KJ to experience a happy childhood; one he felt was stripped away from him. While I empathized with his intentions, I knew the path he was on wasn't the right one, and no amount of reasoning would sway him.

Eventually, I realized I needed to tread carefully around the topic of fatherhood. Continuing to press could create an irreparable divide, something I desperately wanted to avoid. One of his persistent concerns was, why is it acceptable for mothers to stay home while fathers can't? His passion was evident, but I worried about the implications of his decision on his family's future. It was as if he was transforming into someone unrecognizable, and I never imagined he would make a choice that could jeopardize his family's well-being.

My heart was heavy with concern, knowing that Keith's intentions stemmed from love. I just hoped he would one day see the bigger picture and realize there are many ways to show his dedication as a father, ways that don't involve sacrificing the very stability his family needs.

Chapter Eight

Understanding Keith's feelings about his father's situation made it even more puzzling why he chose to step away from a job that not only supported him but also provided for the family he claimed to cherish. He had seen the upheaval that followed his father's job loss, so it was hard for me to grasp why he would risk repeating that scenario. Each time I reached out to Keith, seeking clarity about his choices, he consistently replied, I'm doing it for my son. However, as sincere as that sounded, it began to feel like a vague excuse rather than a solid reason, especially as his demeanor grew increasingly erratic.

In the early days of their marriage, during a time of economic prosperity, Maymay had urged Keith to let her join the workforce. His unwavering response was a firm belief that a wife should not need to work; he wanted to be the sole provider. With some college education under her belt, she had promising potential to find a fulfilling job. Back then, opportunities were blooming, especially with progressive organizations like NASA opening their doors to women. Had he embraced her ambition, she could have accumulated valuable experience that would now ease the family's burden after his job loss. Unfortunately, by the time Keith stepped away from work, many doors had closed.

Though Maymay cherished her moments with Keith, she felt the weight of his decision. She strived to comprehend his motives, but he remained closed off, refusing to discuss anything regarding his feelings, their son, or his past job. As the months went on, the absence of income began to take a toll, unraveling their relationship in ways they never anticipated. With money dwindling and their affection appearing to fade, Maymay realized they needed to shift gears.

After six months of submitting to his decision to leave work, Maymay took a bold step: she informed Keith that she would seek employment. His silence was deafening, prompting her to scour the Times Picayune for opportunities. Times were tough, and securing a well-paying job was proving to be a significant challenge. She understood that she wouldn't earn close to what he used to make, yet Keith seemed unmoved by that reality. While she ventured out to find work, he stayed home caring for KJ, giving their household an aura of stability.

Then came the uplifting moment when Maymay landed a job at Howard Johnson, cleaning rooms. Her excitement was palpable, and to her delight, Keith seemed supportive of this new venture. She recognized that in order for her family to thrive, she needed to contribute financially. With determination and hard work, she envisioned a brighter future ahead, even considering transferring to the casino for better pay.

However, a challenge loomed large: the time her job demanded kept her away from her family, particularly from KJ. This reality weighed heavily on her heart. Whenever she attempted to open a dialogue with Keith about the family dynamics, he insisted that spending time with KJ was paramount. He viewed her job as a sacrifice of precious moments, claiming that the importance of family outweighed any financial gain. Maymay reminded him that her absence from home mirrored his own when he was working, but she found it hard to sway his perspective.

Her shifts began in the early hours and often extended into the late evening. With the demands of her job pulling her away, she felt a growing disconnect with KJ, realizing she had to find a way to reconnect with him. The time Keith spent with their son was fostering a bond that she feared she was losing.

Their conversations often descended into arguments, with Keith accusing Maymay of neglecting their family. Sadly, their disagreements became their primary means of communication, further deepening the rift between them.

He found it hard to accept that she had taken the job out of desperate necessity rather than as an escape from him or KJ. Understanding this dynamic was a struggle for Maymay, especially as she grappled with his perception of her choices. As her frustration swelled, she resolved to work even harder to provide for herself and her child, ironically finding it increasingly challenging to coexist with him. The fabric of their family was fraying before her eyes, and she felt lost in how to mend it.

After a long day of work, Maymay would occasionally stop by to chat with Layla, the weariness evident in her voice. Her job was physically demanding, and it was clear that sometimes she sought refuge in their conversations, grappling with feelings of being overwhelmed. Though she never complained about her work, her unfulfilled desire for a better wage and the strain of her situation were evident.

In the face of these challenges, Maymay persisted with courage and an unwavering commitment to her family. With hope in her heart, she endeavored to navigate the storm, seeking a brighter path for herself and KJ.

Every day when Maymay headed to work, she noticed Keith's anxiousness building up. He would check in on her frequently, and it began to create a cloud of doubt in his mind. He feared that she might leave him for someone else. She sometimes spotted him lingering in the background during her lunch breaks, and even though it made her uncomfortable, she felt discussing it with him would likely lead to more frustration than resolution. Deep down, she sensed that Keith's internal struggle stemmed from guilt about her working while he stayed home. It was an energy she wished he could redirect towards finding a job, an endeavor that could improve their lives dramatically.

Maymay began to observe troubling changes in Keith's behavior towards their son, KJ, and it tugged at her heart. One day, she came home to find KJ covered in bruises on his little legs. When she confronted Keith, he raised his voice, blaming it on the rough-and-tumble nature of little boys, saying, "Boys will be boys." But Maymay knew better. Those bruises reminded her too much of the painful memories of her own childhood when she had been punished with switches. She had promised herself that she would never resort to physical discipline with her children, and she recalled how before their marriage, she and Keith had agreed on a gentler approach to raising KJ. It was becoming painfully clear that he was not the same person she once married.

One morning, just as she was about to leave for work, a heart-wrenching sound made her freeze in her tracks. It was KJ, crying desperately inside the house. Compelled by instinct, she rushed back in only to find Keith hitting KJ with a wooden spoon. She shouted for him to stop, but he insisted he was trying to mold KJ into a "man," asserting that boys shouldn't cry when their mothers left. Maymay swept KJ into her arms, firmly telling Keith that what he was doing was wrong. Hurting a child because he missed his mother wasn't the way. This incident sparked a determination in

Maymay to spend more quality moments with KJ, hoping to mend the bond they shared.

As days went by, she noticed KJ growing increasingly aggressive with his friends, to the point where his peers began to shy away from him. He would lash out when asked to do something he didn't want to. Maymay hoped it was just a phase, choosing patience and love to guide KJ through this challenging time.

However, a moment of concern tipped the scales for Maymay. She heard KJ yelling at his favorite superhero in his room, and when she peeked inside, he hurled the action figure at her. The sight of fear in his eyes sent chills down her spine. He pleaded with her not to hit him, and it broke her heart. Why would I ever do that? she asked, hugging him tightly. He tearfully responded that his daddy hit him all the time.

From that point on, things only seemed to escalate. Maymay noticed that when she came home, Keith would unceremoniously hand KJ off to her and then retreat into the background. He would intentionally bump into KJ, ignoring his child completely. She initially felt a swell of joy when KJ started running to her for hugs upon her arrival, indicating a growing connection. Yet, as time passed, she realized that KJ would cry when she left for work, and her heart sank. Every time she approached Keith about KJ's distress, he'd dismiss it with, he's just a momma's boy. But KJ was only three, and Keith's increasingly hostile attitude toward him left Maymay feeling deeply concerned for her son.

Then came the day that shook her world. She returned home to an empty house, KJ and Keith were nowhere to be found. An overwhelming wave of anxiety washed over her as she frantically searched for them. Desperate and panicked, she came to her friend's house, tears streaming down her face, seeking answers. Thankfully, they had some information; Keith had mentioned a trip to his mother for the week, seemingly part of a family outing. But when she reached out to his mother, the absence of KJ only intensified her fear. She completely unraveled, running around and shouting her fears that KJ was in danger.

Despite the calm assurances from her friends that Keith loved his son and that there was no cause for alarm, Maymay remained determined. She felt an instinctual belief that her son was at risk, and no amount of reasoning could sway her. It was astounding to them how the man they had seen enveloped in love for his family could provoke such fear in her. But Maymay continued to trust her gut feelings, intent on protecting her child with unwavering resolve.

She initially felt a heavy burden of guilt about the situation at home, thinking that encouraging Keith to seek help earlier might have made a difference. However, after some time, she gathered her thoughts and openly shared the challenges they had been facing together. It was a courageous step, and it really helped us understand their journey.

When she first began working, things were going good; Keith was happy being home, and she was happy bringing in a little money. He and KJ welcomed her home every day with a smile, dinner on the table, and sometimes flowers. She recalled the day she opened the door and Keith was standing there in his birthday suit. Of course, when you are not expecting something like that, it's a shock to your system. He had taken their son to his mother's so they could have a night alone. She was so exhausted she couldn't give him the attention he needed. After slowly removing her clothes and laying her on the bed, he began massaging her back with warm oil. As the oil was being poured on her back, she felt all the aches and pains exiting her body. It felt so good she wanted to turn over, grab him and make love to him like they hadn't done in a long time. The more he rubbed her back the harder it was for her to stay conscious.

The next thing she remembered it was morning and he was nowhere to be found. He went over to his mothers to get KJ, and when he returned, she could tell he was upset. She tried to explain she had a hard day, but he didn't believe her. That was the first time he accused her of spending time with someone else. He told her he planned the surprise to see what would happen. He concluded that she was wore out from being with another man, and not because she worked long hours. Maymay couldn't understand how he came to that conclusion. After all, on pay day she handed him her check, and he could see the hours she put in, but he still accused her of falsifying her time sheet. There was nothing she could do to ease his mind, so she stopped trying.

She saw the turning point in her relationship as the moment her work hours increased. While she willingly accepted the overtime to help tackle their financial situation, the weight of their bills was heavy. With the pantry barely stocked and the mortgage in danger of default, the stress was unbelievable. Despite the looming threat from the bank, it felt like Keith was focused solely on her absence from home. He frequently expressed his frustration about how much time she spent away from the family.

Every time she worked late, she made it a priority to call him, providing updates on when she would be home. She wanted to avoid leaving him in the dark, waiting at the table with uncertainty. But instead of alleviating the tension, her calls often turned into arguments. It became unbearable; to prevent those confrontations, she sometimes had to hang up. Yet, through it all, she stayed committed to her hope of keeping her family together.

Keith seemed oblivious to the demands of her job, often contrasting her situation with his own, claiming that he didn't spend as much time away from the family. It felt as though he disregarded the fact that he earned significantly more than she did, making her struggles seem trivial in his eyes.

The day she received her promotion to management was monumental; she could hardly contain her excitement. This was a milestone she had worked hard for, aiming to reach this goal within two years. To celebrate, she stopped at Pizza Palace, his favorite, to pick up a large combo for dinner. She imagined the joy of sharing her success with him, thinking she would be home soon.

But when she walked through the door, Keith's reaction took her by surprise. He bolted upright, startling her and causing her to drop the pizza. At first, she felt threatened, but as she focused, she recognized his anger. He shouted,

> Where have you been? I called your job, and they said you left hours ago. Where in the hell have you been?

Overwhelmed, she didn't have a chance to explain before he stormed out.

As she picked up the fallen pizza and placed it on the table, a wave of disappointment washed over her. On what should have been one of the happiest days of her life, she found herself celebrating alone. After hours of solitude, Keith returned, and they finally talked about her day. To her surprise, he enveloped her in a warm hug, kissed her, and expressed his pride in her accomplishment. That night, they connected like never before, rekindling a spark that had dimmed over time. Recalling those moments brought a radiant smile to her face, it was pure bliss.

Maymay paused, her eyes distant as she reminisced, a soft smile spreading across her lips. Layla laughed, breaking Maymay's trance, and she shared her belief that things would improve from there. For a while, they did. They engaged in conversations about their future, something that had been missing for far too long. Keith seemed happier, and he finally stopped nagging her about her late hours. The bond between Keith and KJ appeared to strengthen as well.

However, one night, when she had to pull an all-nighter due to the night supervisor needing to attend a family emergency, she reached out to Keith. Though he initially took the news well, things soon changed. He slipped back into his old patterns, and the connection they had reignited started to fade away. Confused, she couldn't comprehend what had triggered this change. Keith began spending more time away from home, often leaving as soon as she walked in the door, his whereabouts unknown. Concern began to creep in; she couldn't shake the feeling that something was seriously amiss.

Throughout this turmoil, she turned down countless invitations from others who expressed interest in her, firmly believing in her commitment to her marriage. In her heart, she thought their partnership was unbreakable. Yet, with each passing day, she felt increasingly isolated, as if she were living a single life while standing beside the man she vowed to be with forever.

Even though Keith insisted that the woman he was involved with was simply a friend, it was clear to her that he wasn't being fully truthful. Unable to let him walk away without understanding more, she decided to follow him, and sure enough, he headed to her house. When he knocked on the door, a little boy answered and jumped into his arms with glee. Seeing the joy on the child's face filled her with sadness; it had been far too long since KJ had experienced moments of true happiness with his father. Although part of her wanted to confront him, she ultimately chose to return home to be with her son, knowing that was where she truly belonged.

The story that Maymay shared left me puzzled; I simply couldn't believe that Keith would physically harm his family or deliberately drive them apart. Having known him for most of my life, I knew how much he cherished the idea of family. The thought of him having an affair was nearly impossible to digest. I was curious about this mysterious woman. Keith and I had spent so much time together, yet I had never heard anything about her. While his recent behavior had indeed been a little off, the notion of him being with someone else was shocking. His deep affection for Maymay made it hard to understand why he would risk damaging their relationship by making her believe there was someone else.

The urge to talk to him and get clarity was strong, but attempts to discuss his family situation usually resulted in hostility. It left me bewildered, not knowing what thoughts were running through his mind. He was spiraling, seemingly on a path to destroy everything he held dear, and it left me feeling helpless. The bond we once had, where he confided in me freely, had faded as he increasingly shut me out.

One heartfelt conversation stood out; it was when Keith opened up about wanting to return to work but feeling trapped. It was akin to someone on the brink of starvation who, despite their yearning to eat, simply could not. His belief that nothing could change his situation deeply troubled me, and the sadness laced in his voice was a chilling reminder of his fragile state.

Keith's complaints escalated, causing him to suspect our mutual friend Devell of being KJ's father. I was taken aback, as this seemed entirely out of the blue. We had all grown up together, and I couldn't fathom where this idea originated. I wondered if Keith thought that Maymay harbored lingering feelings for Devell. After confiding his fears, Keith seemed to sink even deeper into his own turmoil. He began disappearing for days on end, refusing visitors when he was home, and it became increasingly clear that he was struggling to cope. The story Maymay shared about his mistreatment of their family was troubling and unnerving.

Maymay left our house heartbroken, still worried about Keith's potential to harm their son. When she got home, she found a message on her answering machine from him, saying they would be back in a couple of days as he needed time to reflect on his life. Although a part of her felt relief to hear from him, she couldn't shake the feeling that something was genuinely wrong with her husband.

After hearing Maymay's perspective and reflecting on our conversations, I felt a strong urge to reach out to Keith the next time we were together. I was determined to understand his side of the story, to bring some clarity into this chaotic situation, and hopefully find a way to support him through this challenging time. My goal was to foster open communication and understanding, believing that together, we could navigate this difficult chapter.

The next morning, when Keith walked in, Maymay eagerly asked about his mother, keen to hear how she was doing. It turned out he hadn't spoken to her yet. He casually mentioned that she was okay and still asleep when he left. Sensing an opportunity to facilitate a connection, Maymay walked over to the phone and, with a friendly smile, called his mother, handing the phone to him. It was clear that he was taken aback by the unexpected turn of events. As he began talking with his mother, his expression shifted dramatically, and frustration slowly crept onto his face. Maymay quickly recognized that his anger arose from a revelation, he and his mother had been caught in a web of dishonesty.

After ending the call, Keith slammed the phone down and approached her, irritation radiating from him. Maymay instinctively took a step back, uncertain about how he would react. Although he had pushed her before, this time, his demeanor suggested he was feeling particularly volatile. Fearful, she shielded her eyes with her hands, not wanting to witness what might unfold. She heard his footsteps draw closer, only to have him walk away instead. When she cautiously opened her eyes, she saw him standing by the door. In a decisive tone, he announced that he wasn't heading to his mother's house before slamming the door shut.

After that encounter, whenever he left the house, arguments often erupted about where he was going. Maymay quickly came to the realization that engaging in these arguments wasn't leading anywhere fruitful, so she decided to let him go. Once he left, she found herself in tears, grappling with the question of what she could have done differently to make him stay. Yet, as time passed, these departures strangely brought a sense of relief to the household. Eventually, she could sense when Keith was ready to leave, prompting her to initiate disagreements just to make it easier for him to go. It might sound unhealthy, but she felt a certain resignation, it was his choice if he wanted to pursue someone else.

During this time, Keith began receiving a flurry of mysterious phone calls. He consistently brushed them off, claiming he was looking for work and receiving callbacks. The first time he used that excuse, Maymay felt a wave of relief wash over her, hopeful that he was finally taking steps to return to work and restore some normalcy to their lives. Perhaps she could even consider cutting down her hours or quitting altogether. She was determined that if Keith secured a job, she would do everything in her power to mend their relationship. With renewed focus, she reduced her work hours, woke up early to prepare breakfast, and made him lunches for his supposed interviews. At times, she managed to come home early to cook dinner, ensuring a warm meal awaited him after a long day. Keith seemed to brighten up with these changes and began spending precious time with KJ, moments they hadn't shared in a long while.

However, a few months later, as she began to ask him about his interviews, Keith's agitation was intense. Maymay couldn't comprehend why he was upset until it dawned on her that he hadn't actually pursued any job opportunities; it was just another façade. Realizing this was a turning point, she understood it was time for her to take decisive action. She recognized that there wasn't a family to restore if he had already let it slip away.

With newfound determination, Maymay dove headfirst into her work, taking on as much overtime as possible. There were days she dedicated ten to fifteen hours to her job, starting her day at six in the morning and often returning home well after midnight. She was aware that this heavy workload bothered Keith, but she felt resolute, if he wanted her home more often, he needed to step up and find a job.

She held onto the hope that her hard work would lead to improvements. If she could just earn enough, they wouldn't have to worry about paying bills or how much food they had in the house. However, she ultimately confronted the tough reality that money alone couldn't solve their deeper issues. With a heavy heart, Maymay accepted that she and KJ might soon find themselves navigating this challenging journey alone. But she was ready to face whatever came next with resilience and strength.

Things had shifted in her life, and she found herself in a situation that felt all too familiar to many. Although she and Keith, were no longer intimate, she sensed an undercurrent of tension that seemed to permeate her interactions with men around her. It was almost as if she were emitting a signal that attracted attention, reminiscent of a moth drawn to a flame. From the very start of her job, she established her boundaries, clarifying that she was happily married and not seeking any romantic entanglements. Yet, as time passed, she became aware that more men were directing their attention towards her. Some even made bold statements like,

> I can make you very happy, or you deserve a good man who will take care of you.

Among these admirers, she found herself particularly drawn to a charming young man named Jerry. He stood tall and handsome, his quiet demeanor often punctuated by laughter that could brighten her day for hours. One day, during a casual conversation, Jerry couldn't help but notice that something seemed off and asked if she was okay. This was during a particularly trying moment, after a heated argument with Keith, and she felt overwhelmed by the tension at home, especially concerning their son. The temptation to share her heart with Jerry was strong, but she held back. After all, she still loved Keith deeply and couldn't imagine being with anyone else.

Keith had been receiving mysterious phone calls, purportedly work-related, which were becoming more frequent and increasingly troubling. One evening, she picked up the phone and was taken aback by the sound of a woman's voice on the other end. A sickening recognition washed over her as she realized it was Fran, a name she had come to associate with distrust. When confronted about the call, Keith flatly denied it, calling her paranoid and suggesting a mix-up had occurred. His excuses were always elaborate, even going so far as to claim that the caller was reaching out for her.

The pattern continued, with late-night calls becoming a regular occurrence. As she lay in bed, she often heard Keith talking in a tone that was light and carefree, a stark contrast to the strain in their own interactions. It was painful to acknowledge the warmth in his voice that hadn't been directed towards her in ages. Frustrated, she couldn't sit idle anymore and decided to confront him about the calls. To her dismay, he remained evasive, continuing to deny any wrongdoing while the calls persisted like clockwork.

One night, she was jolted from sleep by the familiar murmur of his voice. Sure enough, when she quietly approached the room and flipped on the light, she caught him mid-conversation, laughing softly. His reaction to her presence was telling; he froze, clearly caught off guard and momentarily shocked. The joviality faded from his expression, and for an instant, she could see the depth of his panic. She simply wanted to reassure him that she wasn't losing her mind. But instead of engaging, he hung up the phone and walked past her without acknowledging her, slipping out of the house as if nothing had happened.

In that moment, an overwhelming realization washed over her, this marriage might be unraveling before her eyes. The emotions inside her were swirling; she felt an intense anger that caught her off-guard, mixed with the sadness of realizing how far apart they had drifted. And then, a gnawing fear about the unknown paths ahead for both of them. Even amid the anguish he had caused, her concern for his well-being remained. She found herself analyzing their challenges, contemplating whether she had played a part in their situation. In the end, the only fault she could attribute to herself was her unwavering commitment to preserve their family.

After a few days without him, Keith returned home, and they had a heart-to-heart about everything that had been transpiring. He insisted that the woman on the phone was merely a friend, and there was nothing inappropriate happening. Driven by curiosity and concern, she asked him whether he found happiness in this new friendship and whether he believed it was worth saving their family. To her disbelief, Keith seemed to think their distance was a product of her job responsibilities. This struck her as absurd, she loved him dearly, but they both needed to fulfill their roles to support the family. As those words emerged from her lips, she regretted them immediately, fearing that to Keith, it might sound like nothing more than a complaint. His response was palpable, a shift in the room's energy as he stood up and moved toward the door.

In desperation, she pleaded with him, asking if he was heading to his friend's house. His reaction was disheartening as he glanced back at her but then simply walked out without uttering another word. Yet, amidst this turmoil, she held onto hope, a belief that communication could lead to a rekindling of the love they once shared. Even in the face of uncertainty, she remained committed to understanding and healing, determined to find a way forward.

Chapter Nine

A fter Maymay left, Layla and I had a heart-to-heart about what was happening with her and Keith's relationship. I couldn't help but wonder about Keith; he had a loving wife and a beautiful son, what more could he want? Fatherhood was something he had longed for, ever since he was a child dreaming of spending more time with his father. When KJ was born, it seemed like the missing piece had finally fallen into place for them. I knew how excited Keith was to embrace his knew life, believing it was the key to their happiness and fulfillment. So, it was hard for me to wrap my head around the idea that he might think KJ wasn't his son, but instead the result of an affair between Maymay and Devell.

There was a day when I expressed to Layla how I thought it was utterly ridiculous for Keith to doubt KJ's paternity. She gave me a knowing smile and said,

You don't know, do you?

In that moment, my heart raced. It felt like she was hinting at something truly shocking. All the words in my head must have flown out through my ears, because there was nothing there. I just stared at her, utterly shocked. Her expression suggested I was missing out on something crucial, and I desperately wanted her to reassure me that it wasn't true. When she remained silent, I blurted out,

Are you saying she had an affair? I can't believe it; she cheated on Keith?

With a shake of her head, Layla clarified,

Well, not exactly, but KJ isn't Keith's biological child. Maymay was actually artificially inseminated. They tried to conceive naturally, but it didn't work out. The doctor implanted Keith's sperm directly into her, and when that didn't succeed, they had to use a donor. So, in reality, KJ is not biologically his. I think that's why Keith left his job; he wanted to create a strong bond between him and the baby.

As I absorbed her words, it felt like my brain was trying to translate a completely foreign language. I asked her since Keith knew about this, and why, if so, he was causing such drama. I thought to myself, how could he keep this from me, his best friend for life? When I asked Layla how she found out, she explained that Maymay had confided in her from the get-go. Keith was adamant about keeping it a secret because he didn't want anyone looking at him or KJ with judgement.

This was a lot to process for me. I felt my heart racing as I sat down, trying to come to terms with this new reality. After a moment, I exclaimed,

> Layla, I'm not just anyone, I'm your husband and Keith's best friend. You should have told me sooner, especially when things started getting disillusion between them. I could've help him maneuver through this, how could you keep this from me all these years? So, what you are saying is that Keith and Maymay planned to have KJ this way?

Layla shared that she made a promise to Maymay and didn't think it was a big deal, she figured Keith and I had the same deal, so it was nothing to talk about. For Maymay, what truly mattered was that she and Keith had a child to cherish and love. They both understood that Keith couldn't have children, but that didn't stop their desire to start a family. They believed wholeheartedly that their love was more than enough for any child. Maymay had discussed their fertility journey with Layla, who encouraged them to pursue their dreams if they both agreed, promised that she wouldn't share this information with anyone.

As I began to understand the situation, I wondered why he would suggest that Devell was KJ's father. Layla felt that maybe he was using that as a way to mask the truth about his life. While I could see her point, my mind was racing and struggling to make sense of it all. If they had agreed on the fertility process together, why was he distancing himself from his own family? My thoughts spun in circles, trying to convince me that Layla must be mistaken, but I knew deep down she had no reason to lie.

She encouraged me to have a conversation with Keith, to see what was really on his mind. But I hesitated, how could I approach him about this sensitive topic if he wanted to keep it hidden? Layla recognized that Keith was struggling, and suggested that talking to him could be a great opportunity for him to open up to someone he loved and trusted, which could and return help him maneuver through his struggles.

I felt a mix of anxiety and determination. Keith needed support, and maybe it was time for me to step up and be there for him. After all, friendship sometimes meant navigating the tough conversations, and I was more than willing to lend a listening ear and offer my support.

I found myself reflecting on the nature of best friendships and how they thrive on openness, especially when it involves significant moments in our lives. This thought made me reconsider our friendship, something I had never done before, I started to think about how I would feel if I were in his position. Honestly, I felt I would have shared the news because they are like family to me. It was a tough realization that the same might not be true for them, and I felt a bit hurt. However, I quickly reminded myself that this isn't about me; it's about supporting them.

I was eager to connect with Keith, but I learned from Maymay that she had not seen him for a little over a week. He had been spending time with his mother, because was wasn't feeling too good these days. His return was uncertain, so I awaited his comeback. When he finally did return, I struggled to navigate the conversation toward his situation with his family.

It seemed like when he returned things seem to be better between them, but it all felt apart at football Sunday, which was at his house this week. Keith, Devell, and I were enjoying the Saints game against the Falcons. The Saints were on a winning streak, which Keith would always be over excited about, but I could sense something was troubling him. He made some teasing comments towards Devell, which seemed out of character.

> Hey pretty boy, too bad you are not still playing, everyone thought you were a winner, but look at you. If I'm not mistaken, you made a bet with me and Dee that you would make it to the NFL. Do you remember what that bet was? I believe you owe us one hundred dollars, and an ass kissing, so pay up.

We were all sharing laughs and trying to lighten the mood, despite the tough situation. It was surprising to see him react that way, but with everything he was dealing with, it made some sense. Devell, however, seemed really shaken, it was clear he wanted to stand up and knock the shit out of him, especially since he was still sensitive about being pushed out of football.

I remember the game that crushed his dreams, when chaos erupted in the stands, and everyone began scrambling to safety. Just as the ball was snapped to him, Devell and his teammates turned to see what was going on. Unfortunately, the opposing team didn't hold back and Devell ended up caught off guard. He stood there, and out of nowhere, someone hit him low, causing his knee to give out. Later on, we learned that Keith had instigated the fight, claiming he was defending Maymay. While I know Devell never blamed him, I could tell he wasn't thrilled about it being brought up.

Just when Devell was about to share his thoughts, KJ entered the room, and that's when things took a shameful turn. Keith, who was clearly overwhelmed, suddenly started yelling at KJ, leaving everyone stunned. KJ, clearly caught off guard, cautiously moved towards the TV, and just in that moment, Williams made a sixty-yard touchdown run, The excitement of the game only heightened Keith's frustration. I couldn't believe what I was witnessing as he grabbed KJ's arm,

> It's all because of you my life is so miserable. Why did you have to come and mess up my life? You are not my son,

As Devell jumped to his feet, Keith stared him down as if to say, I know he is your son. He then looked down at KJ,

> I don't care what your momma says, I know who your daddy.

After recalling what Layla had shared with me, it was heartbreaking to see KJ, once full of confidence, become stiff with fear as he faced Keith's anger. I felt a surge of concern; I never imagined Keith would act this way, even with all that had happened between him and Maymay. As Keith shook KJ, his gaze remained fixed on Devell. I noticed the shocked expression on Devell's face; it was clear he wanted to intervene, but he was rooted to the spot. I sprang forward and grabbed his shoulders from behind. Despite my efforts, he continued shaking the boy, so I punched him several times to the back of his head.

Dropping the child onto the floor, Keith turned to face both of us, his fists clenched. I could see that he was out of control. As he raised his fist above his head, he seemed to be looking right through me. But as his eyes began to focus, he slowly lowered his hands to his sides. Tears welled in his eyes, and shame washed over his face. It was as if he felt embarrassed for being out of control in front of us.

He then walked away, stopping in front of KJ, who lay on the floor, crying. For a moment, I thought he might pick him up and try to comfort him, but instead, he stepped over him. Just then, Maymay burst into the room, yelling.

That's the last time you ever put your hands on my child, get the hell out of my house right now. You know what? You're right; you're not his father, and he needs someone who can love and support him like a real father. The idea of him being raised in an environment that doesn't value him is heartbreaking. No child should have to endure that. So, git out and leave us along.

After Keith left, I felt bad for Maymay and KJ. Not only did she have to hear such vicious statements about her child, but he tried to make it look like she was whoring around, knowing how KJ came about. When she stared into my eyes, I could see her pain and that pain was transferred to me; I felt water building in my eyes so I looked away. She walked over, picked up KJ, and he began crying. We could see that she was too hurt to talk to us about what had occurred so we went after Keith to talk to him about what he had done to them. Devell said if he found Keith, he would kill him. It took me a while to calm him, but I did and we went our separate ways.

I caught up with Keith at the Hi Note, a cozy little bar on Forstall Street, just a stone's throw away from his place. I had a feeling he'd be there since it's the perfect spot for anyone looking for a friendly ear. Sandra genuinely listens to everyone, and by the time you leave, you either feel lighter after sharing your troubles or ready to let loose. I really wanted to be there for Keith. It's clear he had been through something tough to say those hurtful things, and I wanted to show him that he's not alone in his pain.

When I got there, he was sitting at the bar. As I got close to him, the picture of Maymay's face and KJ lying on the floor entered my mind. I could feel the rage flowing through my veins; it started in my head and made its way down to my feet. She was like a sister to me and no one was going to do anything to hurt her, no one, not even her husband, or my best friend. With that thought I must have lost my mind, I grabbed him off the stool, and hurled him against the wall. I flung his body over and over yelling something, which I can't remember. I just remember throwing him back and forth with the same rage, the same way he did the boy. He did nothing to stop me because I figured he felt bad for what he had done to them. His feeling bad wasn't enough for me; I wanted him to feel pain. I wanted him to feel as much physical pain as the mental pain I saw on Maymay's face.

The bartender grabbed me and shouted for me to stop, but I continued kicking his ass. I threw him on the ground and began kicking him with all my strength. I noticed he was no longer moving and thought I had killed him, which brought me back to my senses. He slowly looked up at me with blood coming from his mouth and nose, he was holding his ribs as if some of them were broken, and I could see his eyes watering almost spilling out. I knew the tears weren't for what I had done to him but for what he had done to his family. All of a sudden, I got an aching feeling in my chest. I felt I was no better than him because I had lost control of myself too. I walked over to him, placed my hand on his shoulder and apologized for my behavior.

He took a seat on a stool, his head bowed, with a stream of blood trickling from his nose. The bartender kindly offered Keith some napkins and suggested he tilt his head back. After a little while, the bleeding subsided, and he cautiously wiggled his nose to check for any breaks. Standing up, he stretched a bit to make sure everything felt alright. I settled beside him and wanted to understand what was troubling him, particularly his actions and words towards his family. He met my gaze and a faint smile graced his lips, but then he glanced down at his feet, his voice soft yet sincere.

> I love Maymay and my son dearly, but she deceived me, just look at KJ and tell me what you see. I never intended to hurt him, but the truth is, she wasn't honest with me.

His honesty was palpable, and I felt a wave of compassion for him. It was clear that he was grappling with deep feelings.

> Look Keith, we're talking about an innocent child, and the difficulties you're facing with Maymay shouldn't spill over onto him. He's just a little one; how is he supposed to understand or defend himself in this chaos? You're his father, the one person he should feel safe and secure trusting. You've told me you don't see yourself as his father right now.

> Well, I'm not his father, you know? Maymay made me believe that he was conceived through artificial

114

insemination, but it turns out that wasn't true. She had an affair.

That's a tough truth to face, but your words were incredibly painful. Even if KJ doesn't recall this moment later, Maymay will always remember how hurtful that conversation was.

I know it might be hard to see from where you're standing.

What do you mean? I can't help but feel that you're overlooking how deep your words can cut. You hurt someone you claim to love, and it's difficult to justify such actions.

I felt crushed when she told me the truth. She was honest with me, looking me straight in the eye.

So, she was honest with you. And now what? Is there any justification for the pain you caused? I just don't understand how you believed that was the right way to respond. I'm really struggling to see your side.

You know, Maymay and I had been dreaming of starting a family for years. We tossed around options like artificial insemination and adoption. I wanted to adopt, but she had her heart set on giving birth to our child, and in support, I agreed. That's part of why I made the choice to leave my job; I wanted to build that bond with KJ and show him that I love him as his father.

I hear you, but it sounds like you're in a situation where you know he's not your biological child.

But she lied to me, I know who the father really is.

Who's that? I'm curious to know,

Devell is KJ's father. Maymay had an affair, and he is the one.

I find that hard to believe, everyone knows they dated way back in high school. After graduation, he went into the service, and they lost touch. What makes you think he's involved now?

As I said, she admitted it to me.

Did she specifically say that Devell is KJ's father? I really can't accept that. It's clear how much Maymay loves you; she always has, I'm not sure why she would say something that feels so far from the truth. If you genuinely trusted and loved her, I think you'd see it's just not accurate.

I do love and trust her. I really do, but when I look at KJ, I can't help but see his resemblance to Devell. That's the reality for me. I challenge you to look at him again, keep what I've told you in mind, and then make your own judgment. I believe with all my heart that there's a connection.

I hear you, but I have to say that it feels like a contradiction. You claim to love and trust her, but then there's a "but" attached to it. Can you see how that creates confusion? It's like there's a wall between your words and your feelings.

I really think you should go back, look at KJ with fresh eyes, and then let's have another chat. There may be something you can uncover that will help us both understand what's happening here. I'm genuinely here for you as you process this

Leaving the bar and heading back to Keith's house, I found myself replaying our conversation in my mind. I could see how deeply he believed what he was saying, and honestly, that unsettled me because I found myself believing him too. After all, we had been friends for ages, and he had never steered me wrong. As I walked, a wave of emotions washed over me. It felt like a tug-of-war between my loyalty to him and my affection for her. It was confusing, I didn't know who to trust. He had never explained the details surrounding her pregnancy, and neither had she. I felt caught in this emotional maze, trying to make sense of everything. I genuinely cared for both of them, but something drew me to her. Maybe it was her vulnerability; if he couldn't be her hero, I felt a strong urge to protect her.

As I stepped into the house, I saw Maymay cradling KJ in her arms, rocking him back and forward. For a brief moment, my heart skipped a beat, I thought maybe he wasn't breathing. But as I got closer, I realized he was just peacefully sleeping. When Maymay looked up at me, I felt a rush of surprise. KJ's resemblance to Devell was uncanny, she must have sensed my shock, because she immediately asked me what was the matter, and wanted to know if Keith was okay. I assured her he was fine, as I was still trying to wrap my head around everything. While staring at KJ I couldn't help but see what Keith was talking about.

> It's just... it's true, isn't it? Look at that little boy. I wouldn't have believed it if I hadn't seen him myself. How could you put Keith in this position?

Her expression turned serious as she replied,

> You've talked to Keith about KJ, haven't you? What he said is true.

I couldn't help but feel a wave of frustration.

> But how could you do this to him?

> What do you mean?".

> An affair with Devell. How could you?

> Dee, I swear on everything, I didn't sleep with Devell. You know me better than anyone; I need you to believe me. If KJ were Devell's son, do you really

think I'd be with Keith? I love Keith, and you know that. Why would I jeopardize everything for an affair?

I was puzzled and asked why did she agreed with him?

She took a deep breath and followed up with a heartfelt explanation.

> When KJ was just a couple of months old, I noticed he was starting to resemble Devell. At first, I shrugged it off because babies have that tendency, and he also had Keith's features. But as he grew, the resemblance to Devell became more apparent, and honestly, it sparked all kinds of questions from Keith. We ended up in repeated arguments over it. One day, feeling overwhelmed, in anger I blurted out that Devell could be KJ's father. That only made things worse; he wanted details. I tried to backtrack, insisting I only said it to stop the fighting, but he didn't buy it.

> Why would you say something like that if you knew KJ looked like Devell?

I asked, my curiosity piqued.

> I don't know, I guess I was just exhausted from the constant conflict. It felt like it was all we ever talked about, and I wanted it to end. I realize now that saying that was wrong, but it was all just too much. It seemed like every day, he accused me of being with

Devell, and I thought maybe agreeing with him would put an end to the accusations, but it only made things worse. My attempts to convince him it was a lie were falling on deaf ears."

Every word she said filled me with a mix of understanding and empathy.

You know, if you really want to put this whole situation to rest, a simple blood test might be a good step forward.

But why should I put my son through that? I haven't done anything wrong. KJ and I are not the issue here.

Think of it this way: doing the test could save your marriage.

Isn't marriage supposed to be built on love and trust? Keith doesn't seem interested in working on this; his actions show a lack of either.

I understand, but given the circumstances, especially if you really do see a resemblance to Devell, it would be wise to consider every option to clear the air.

Are you suggesting I invite Devell to join me for a blood test? That's just not reasonable. Asking him to do this implies there's a chance he is the father. Once again, I want to emphasize that Devell and I did not have an affair.

Maymay, I'm not saying Keith's beliefs are valid; I'm only suggesting it's an easy solution. Why not reach out to Devell, explain what's happening, and ask for his support for the sake of your family? If your heart is set on making your marriage work, this could be a way forward. I bet Devell would be more than willing to help because he's a true friend.

But how can you ask a friend to do something like that? Imagine how it would feel if someone accused you of fathering their child and then requested a blood test to sort it all out. You'd think they were out of their mind,

Honestly, if it were to help a friend's family, I'd step up. If I had nothing to hide, it would be no problem. I would do anything for a friend.

You know, I really don't want to go down this road, but I see I have no choice. I can't keep living like this.

After our chat, I made my way back to the bar, feeling the weight of everything. As I walked, I contemplated how to approach Keith. I knew mentioning Maymay's plan wouldn't help; it would only make things worse. When I arrived, I placed my hand on his shoulder, hoping to bring some positivity into the conversation. He looked up and asked,

What did you see? I want you to look me in the eye and tell me I'm a liar.

His expression made it clear he was hoping I'd reassure him that KJ didn't resemble Devell. I tried my best to be convincing, but I could see he wasn't buying it. He jumped off his stool and shouted,

> Be real with me, I know you see what I see every day: that boy looks just like Devell,

For a moment, I was speechless, but eventually, I managed to reply,

> Keith, I took a close look at him, and honestly, he looks like an ordinary little boy. He even has some features that resemble me a bit. Do you think I could be the father?

> Of course not, But I'll tell you this: he might look a bit like you and a bit like me, but that boy strongly resembles Devell.

> Okay, let's just say you're right, he looks like him. What does that mean for you? Are you considering leaving your family? Confronting Devell? Blaming Maymay? What's your next move?

Keith hung his head.

> It's his child, isn't it? Maymay must have told you the truth.

No, she said she could never be unfaithful to you, and I genuinely believe her. She's a wonderful woman, and deep down, you should know that. It's hard to see you struggling like this. Remember how good Maymay has always been to you? Rather than turning your back on her, I encourage you to gather your thoughts, talk to your wife, ask for her forgiveness, and hope that one day, this will just be a distant memory for your family.

As I left the bar, I noticed he was deep in thought but still unsure. At this point, I felt a sense of hope that Maymay would find a way to get the blood test, putting an end to the doubt once and for all.

Hidden Emotions

Chapter Ten

aymay agreed that she should bring clarity to the situation she was facing, so she approached Devell with hope in her heart. However, she was totally surprised when he respectfully declined her request. Her mind raced with thoughts, and she felt an overwhelming urge to persuade him to reconsider. After all, this felt crucial. Devell raised a valid concern about the emotional turmoil that might arise if the blood test yielded inconclusive results, and while she found it hard to comprehend at that moment, she understood her request was significant. Yet, with Keith convinced that Devell might be KJ's biological father, Maymay felt determined that the test was the only means to resolve the tension that had permeated their lives for years.

When Devell cautiously proposed the idea that Keith may have a connection to KJ as his father, Maymay was momentarily baffled. Given the meticulous process she underwent to conceive, she couldn't fathom where such a thought could originate. Nonetheless, Devell's question lingered in her mind as he sought clarity about the situation.

> It's simply not possible. I'm only trying to prove that you're not the father, that's the reassurance he needs. Once we have the test results, I truly believe things will get better between us. This uncertainty has cast a shadow over our lives for far too long, and it's time to bring closure to this chapter.

As she opened up about her struggles, she felt a pressure forming in her head, it felt as if it was going to explored leaving matter all over. The thought of someone who professed to care for her, would find reason to deny their such crucial help was unconceivable. Devell seemed to have reasons he wanted to share, but he felt it was essential that the two of them came together to hear the truth. She realized how much she longed for his support, and her curiosity grew. There was a sense of urgency within her, a need to understand what held him back.

Her thoughts began to spiral, and a wave of anxiety washed over her. But then a startling thought gripped her: What if Devell were a donor, and what if KJ was indeed his son? The realization took her breath away. It felt surreal, given that Maymay and Keith had both agreed not to involve anyone from their circle in their journey. The more she considered it, the more unnerved she became, especially since the donor's description might align closely with Devell. The idea sent her mind racing, if Devell was truly KJ's father, what would that mean for her marriage? Would she pursue a relationship with Devell, or would it be time to leave with her son in search of a new life?

When they convened to discuss the situation, Devell expressed the importance of addressing this together. Maymay held her breath, hoping for clarity and fearing the worst. She looked at Devell intently, bracing herself for the weighty conversation that was about to unfold.

Shortly after we moved into the neighborhood, I discovered something about my father,

Devell began, a heaviness in his voice.

Through the years, my real father and I have shared countless memories.

Maymay felt a swirl of confusion, what was he trying to convey? But she decided to remain open and attentive.

Keith, I love you deeply, and my intention has always been to protect you. But now, it's time for the truth: we are brothers. We share the same father.

Those words felt like a whirlwind inside her, the reality was dizzying. She struggled to grasp how this revelation connected to the answers she sought. Certainty slipped through her fingers as she tried to comprehend the implications of Devell's statement.

> Keith, I wanted to tell you for so long, but the timing never felt right. That's why KJ carries some of my features, and if you look closely, you'll find he resembles you even more.

As the gravity of the moment settled in, Maymay felt a flicker of hope amidst the chaos. Perhaps this revelation was the turning point they all needed.

> Keith, I completely understand why you might find this hard to believe, but I encourage you to talk to your mom, she can share the full story. Do you remember our chats at the barber shop with your dad? Those encounters were really special to me.

> There's something I wanted to clarify. One day, after your dad dropped me off, I overheard a conversation between him and my mom. Your dad mentioned that things had been tough with your mom, they were separated during that time. When he found out about your mom's pregnancy, they decided to come back together.

> What's important to note is that my mom was also pregnant then but chose not to tell your dad, believing it might complicate things. When my parents married, they were upfront about my

situation, knowing I wasn't his biological child. They hoped for a fresh start.

Your dad has always been a big part of my life, which is why I spent so much time at your place. I kept this secret for a long time, but I'm a bit nervous about the test revealing our connection. I hope we can navigate this together.

What test are you talking about? This is the most preposterous thing I've ever heard, let me try to process the information you have given us. We are brothers and you feel KJ is my son, right. You must be insane. Get the fuck out of here, I don't know what kind of stunt you and Maymay are trying to pull, but you both think I'm stupid. Ok, ok wait a minute, let's say you and I share the same father, which I don't believe, but let's just say for the sake of argument, it's true. Now, on top of that lie you want me to think I'm KJ's father. Man, you must have a set of brass balls. First, you have relations with my wife, then you make up this cockamamie story about my father, and you want me to believe it all. Tell me why I shouldn't take a knife and ram it through your neck right now.

Keith, what I'm telling you is true.

Tell me something Devell, did you go to Tulane University? Are you a doctor? Did you spend ten years in college that no one knows about? Do you know something they don't? I'll tell you something; get your ass out of my house before I kill you.

As Devell left the room, he yelled,

Talk to your mother, she knows. She can tell you I'm not lying. Talk to her that's all I ask of you, talk to her. Keith, you have known me long enough to know I wouldn't lie to you about something so serious. Maymay, you believe me, don't you, you know better than anyone that KJ is not my son. Tell him, make him believe what I'm saying is true.

I don't want to get my family involved in this chaos. Even if Maymay is on your side, it doesn't change the fact that, that child looks like you are the daddy.

Not long after Devell spoke with them, he and I had a heart-to-heart. He shared the story about his father. His father revealed that he hadn't known about his existence until years later. One day, while coming home from work, he spotted Devell playing outside and had a profound realization,

That's my son, I wonder who is his mother.

A few days later, he reached out to Devell's mother, who joyfully confirmed it. From then on, his dad made it a point to visit every now and again after work, eager to spend time with Devell. Devell fondly remembers the day his father introduced him to Keith, telling him that this was his brother.

When Keith's mother first met Devell, she wasn't very welcoming; in fact, she had a tough time warming up to him. However, as time went on, Mrs. Shirley surprisingly opened her heart and embraced Devell into their lives. One pivotal moment came after Devell faced the heartbreaking loss of Mr. Jackson. A significant source of pain for him was that he hadn't been mentioned in his father's obituary. He felt this was an important chance to affirm his identity, to showcase who he was to his family and the world. When he confided in Keith's mom about his feelings, she told him it wasn't the right moment. Sadly, that moment never came for her. He eventually found peace in the realization that his identity and his father's legacy would remain a mystery to many. Devell had always been honest with me, so I took his words seriously, but I could also understand Keith's skepticism.

Recognizing the challenges ahead, Devell made a tough decision to leave the neighborhood for the good of himself and Maymay. His departure was a bittersweet event; it saddened everyone, except for Keith. In his mind, he believed this departure signified guilt, feeling he had unraveled the truth about them and that Devell wasn't brave enough to confront it. Maymay, with her caring nature, tried to encourage Keith to share his feelings with his mother about what Devell had revealed. Unfortunately, her kind intentions didn't resonate with him.

Maymay found herself in a challenging situation. Since Keith had chosen to withdraw from all communication with his mother about what Devell said, she felt compelled to address the troubling allegations they were facing directly with Mrs. Shirley. It took her several days to muster the courage to have that conversation; she understood that confronting this sensitive topic would be difficult, but sometimes these conversations are essential. With her thoughts organized and determination in her heart, she made her way to her mother-in-law's house to discuss the matter.

However, every time she mentioned Devell's name, it was as if Mrs. Shirley shifted the conversation elsewhere. This redirection only amplified Maymay's determination. In a moment of frustration, she boldly asked her if Keith and Devell really brothers?

The look of surprise on Mrs. Shirley's face spoke volumes. For a fleeting instant, it seemed as if she might offer a confession, but instead, she deftly changed the subject, inquiring about Keith's well-being. Maymay, not willing to let the conversation shift away from the critical issue at hand, reiterated her question,

Are Devell and Keith brothers?

The silence that followed was thick with tension, leaving both women in a state of discomfort.

In a surprising turn, Mrs. Shirley suggested that Maymay should focus on why Keith wasn't working. Maymay locked eyes with Mrs. Shirley, searching for any hint of truth beneath the surface. Although there was no ill intention evident, it was clear that something was being concealed. When Maymay tried to express her worries about Keith's unsettling behavior, Mrs. Shirley seemed to retreat further into her shell. Realizing that her efforts might be in vain, Maymay reluctantly halted her pursuit for answers, feeling the weight of disappointment encumbering her spirit.

As she prepared to leave, Mrs. Shirley once again probed,

What's wrong with Keith? Why isn't he working?

Maymay took a deep breath, hoping for a connection.

I came here seeking clarity, Keith seems to be struggling with something profoundly troubling, something that feels beyond my grasp. I've tried reaching out, but he's become so withdrawn. It's as if bitterness has taken root, distorting his ability to reason. I can't shake the feeling that he's lost himself. He's avoided work, distanced himself from helping at home, and has become a stranger to our son. I feel despair knowing I might lose him, which is the last thing I want. Please, I need your help.

I know for the most part he had a great childhood. I remember when we were young, many kids from the neighborhood love coming over. Yet, I'm at a loss regarding what he is experiencing now. I didn't mean to offend you; I'm simply desperate for answers. I should head home now; thank you for listening.

As Maymay strolled home after the encounter, she couldn't help but feel a sense of epiphany wash over her. If Mrs. Shirley couldn't provide any insight into Keith's unusual behavior, then perhaps they were all trapped in this cycle of confusion. It occurred to her that Keith never got a chance to share his feelings with his mother.

Chapter Eleven

When Devell left the area, Keith was convinced he'd found the proof he needed to justify his feelings and it felt like Devell lacked the courage to stand by his actions. Keith went through a radical change in his self-care routine. He stopped showering, shaving, and even combing his hair, allowing his clothes to become wrinkled and dirty. I still remember the day he approached me; the transformation was astonishing. With his unkempt hair both on his head and face, it was almost uncanny how closely he resembled his father during his last days, in both appearance and demeanor.

I genuinely wanted to reach out to him and discuss the changes I was observing, the ones that mirrored his father's path. However, Keith was resistant, firmly believing that he was living life on his own terms and that I should respect his choices. This led to troubling patterns; he frequently went missing for days at a time without a word to his family. For Maymay, this was especially tough. Even though it seemed their relationship was at a breaking point, she continued to love and care for him deeply. At one point, Keith began inviting female friends over, claiming they were nothing more than people he like hanging out with. This only added to the turbulence in their already strained relationship. Maymay felt overwhelmed by the chaos. I even suggested to Maymay that I take him somewhere to help him realize the impact of his choices, but she hesitated; she believed that once he worked through this tumultuous phase, he would return to her, ready to love again.

While Maymay was at work, Keith threw wild parties, often inviting people who didn't have the best reputations in the neighborhood. Sometimes, the festivities would still be in full swing when Maymay came home, almost as if he had signaled the end of the gathering with her arrival. The aftermath was always shocking; the house would be a complete disaster. One day, Maymay called us for help, completely drained from trying to manage it all alone. When we walked into her home, it was overwhelming, beer bottles, plates of leftover food, and glass scattered everywhere. To our disbelief, Keith's large TV was missing, along with Maymay's two beautiful lamps that had once graced the side tables by the couch. I could feel a surge of anger bubbling inside me, a strong urge to confront him about the mess he had created. But instead, I chose to channel that energy into helping Layla clean up the chaos. We suggested that Maymay consider leaving, but she was steadfast. She truly believed that her love could help pull Keith back to his senses, reasoning that she had done nothing wrong while he was convinced, she accepted his behavior out of guilt for her past with Devell.

I still remember the painful day when Keith's actions led to Maymay being suspended from work. Her boss had already issued several warnings about her tardiness and absences, and Keith was fully aware of the precarious situation. On the morning of her suspension, he erupted into a confrontation about Devell, harshly demanding that she confess to any infidelity. When Maymay tried to walk away, he grabbed her arm and struck her. The following day, she had a black eye, which resulted in her missing three days of work.

When we heard that she had been suspended, Layla and I stopped by to see what happened. When we saw her face, Layla bent over, grabbed her stomach then ran to the bathroom. Maymay's face was swollen and she didn't look like herself. I asked her who did this, but she didn't need to answer because I knew. As I stood there staring at her face, my connection to her became overwhelming. I puffed up like a blow fish and wanted break Keith's neck. As she placed her hands on her face and slowly began gliding them over all the lumps and bumps, my face began tingling. It was as if her hands were stroking my face. All of a sudden, I could feel her pain. I closed my eyes and allowed the strokes to sooth the throbbing. When I opened my eyes, they were staring at me. I guess they could see that something was going on within me. I walked over to the mirror because I had to see where that pain came from, but there was nothing. I wanted to talk to Layla but I didn't know what to say. I had to leave; I had to find him. He was out of control and someone had to stop him. As I walked the street, my mind tried to put in perspective this new connection with Maymay. Did I love her more than I thought? Was I realizing I married the wrong friend? These thoughts were confusing, and I didn't know what to do with them. After walking around the neighborhood for two hours and not finding Keith, I decided to return. I could see the relief on Maymay and Layla's faces when I walked in the door. I guess it was obvious I had not found him because my knuckles weren't bloody and my clothing was intact.

We were delighted to welcome her and KJ into our home for a couple of weeks, hoping that some time away would bring them comfort and support. However, after just one week, we began to see the struggle she was facing. Keith started reaching out, insisting that they return home. He claimed it was just a moment of poor judgment fueled by alcohol, assuring her that things would be different. While we wanted her to stay and feel safe, she felt the urge to go back.

About a month later, we noticed that the troubling patterns continued. Keith would call her at work, urging her to come home with vague claims that something was wrong. When she would arrive, he would often be missing, leaving KJ alone. On another distressing occasion, she called home to hear KJ screaming, and when she inquired, he abruptly hung up. The situation escalated when Keith showed up at her workplace without KJ, insisting he didn't know where their child was. His erratic behavior took a toll on her, leading to missed work and mounting stress.

It became clear that the human mind has its limits. She started to feel as if KJ was at the core of the issue, reminiscing about how joyful life had been before his birth and how beautiful their marriage once was. Gradually, she began to detach from the memories of KJ altogether, calling him "the boy" as a way to mentally distance herself from the pain. This mindset led to her shutting down emotionally, withdrawing from friends and family, and eventually leaving her job. In this challenging period, she neglected both her own well-being and KJ's, transforming from a once vibrant woman into someone who seemed lost. Alcohol became her escape, leaving KJ to navigate life more independently than any child should.

During our visits, we were taken aback to see Maymay dependent on alcohol, a stark contrast to the woman we once knew. When she drank, her behavior turned harsh, especially toward KJ and others around her. This innocent little boy, who had come to know his mother as a source of love, was caught in the crossfire of her struggles. After Keith left, she had poured her heart into giving KJ all the affection he could ever need. Yet now, it felt as though she could hardly bear to be around him. The once joyful, smiling child became increasingly withdrawn, and his beautiful spirit seemed dimmed. In his eyes, you could see the confusion and fear, a profound challenge to explain to a child.

In these moments, all we could do was shower him with love and attention whenever we had the chance, striving to bring back a glimmer of happiness into his life. Together, we hoped to remind him of the joy he still deserved to feel despite the turmoil surrounding him.

Keith often found himself away from home, and it felt like he only returned to stir up tension. The more she tried to cope, the more overwhelming things became. It was disheartening to see her hit such a low point, especially when Keith returned to work, and we hoped this change might bring some positivity, but it didn't.

During our visits, his comments about her appearance and home were still sharp and hurtful. It was as if he failed to see the impact of his words on her well-being.

While he was attempting to engage with the outside world again, it felt like Maymay had lost her spark. It was heartbreaking to witness her struggle, and it seemed Keith remained indifferent to her pain. However, I believe in resilience and the possibility of brighter days ahead for Maymay. With support and love, I knew we can help her regain her strength and find joy once more.

One day Keith was bad mouthing his family while they were sitting in the room with us. That was the last straw; I could no longer pretend she was too drunk to understand what was being said about her and her son. It made me think how slaves must have felt when white folks thought they were too stupid to understand that they were talking about selling their babies to the highest bidder or other atrocities. All of a sudden it dawned on me that I had not defended a very special person. I jumped to my feet and grabbed his dumb ass around the neck. I spoke in a soft tone,

> If you ever talk bad, or put your hands on her again, you won't be able to say nothing bad about no one else because I'm going to rip your tongue out of your mouth and wrap it around your hands so that you can't speak or hit anyone again. Do you understand me? All of this is your fault, and you have the nerve to criticize her, what in the hell are you thinking. After what you've done to them, please.

I thought about what I was doing, and let loose of the grip I had around his neck, then I had to walk away fast. I was so upset that if a smile had appeared on his face, I would have ripped it off. As I left, I turned to say good-bye to Maymay, and noticed she had a partial smile on her face. I gave her a smile and left.

The next time I encountered his troubling behavior; I decided to talk to him about it. His cold demeanor made it a challenge to keep my emotions in check. Despite my frustration, I focused on understanding the situation, especially regarding the violence he directed at Maymay. I asked him why he felt the need to hurt her when he drank. His chilling response took me by surprise: "Because of what she did to me, I drank in order to hit her."

I couldn't believe my ears and felt a wave of disbelief wash over me. I needed a moment to process everything, so I stepped outside, overwhelmed with sadness for him. It hit me hard that our friendship was over. I recognized that if I stayed, I might do something I would regret deeply. For so long, we had thought alcohol was the root of his issues, but it was clear there was much more to unravel. I left with a heavy heart, hoping he would one day find the help he truly needs.

After some time, Keith made the difficult decision to leave his family behind, prompting KJ to take on the brave responsibility of caring for both himself and his mother. Unfortunately, the situation attracted attention from neighbors, who were concerned for KJ's safety. One day, a neighbor witnessed a frightening moment when KJ, in distress, pleaded with his mother to be let down from a window. When the police arrived, KJ was lying on the floor. For a brief period, he was placed in a foster home, but he was soon returned to his mother. Multiple times, Layla and I visited their home and found him hungry and in need of care. We truly wanted to help, but Maymay, resisted our support. I sensed her anger about the fallout with Devell over the blood test, which she believed had inevitably led to the collapse of her marriage. This made it difficult for her to welcome us into KJ's life, as she insisted, we had done enough already.

One of the most unsettling experiences I can recall happened after a long day of shopping. We returned home to find a message from the police department on our answering machine, asking if we knew Maymay and letting us know they needed to speak with us. As we waited for the police to arrive, a wave of worry washed over us. Thoughts like, "What if something happened to KJ? Why didn't they mention both of them? What has she done to him?" raced through our minds. It felt like an eternity until we heard a knock at the door. Layla peered through the peephole and saw the officers standing there, and I could see the hesitation on her face about opening the door, as if not opening it could somehow shield her from bad news. I urged her to open the door, but she was frozen in place. The officer must have heard my voice, as he knocked more urgently. I stepped up, moved her aside, and swung the door open. What a relief it was to see KJ standing next to the officer,

Layla quickly apologized to the officer for taking so long and invited him inside. It was clear that KJ had been crying, and my heart ached for him. The officer explained that Maymay had been arrested for public misconduct and even assaulting an officer just two days before. In the chaos, she didn't mention that she had a child at home. One of the neighbors had spotted KJ outside at three o'clock in the morning, playing as if it was the middle of the day. When asked about his mother, KJ replied that he didn't know where she was. The neighbor took care of him for a couple of days, hoping that Maymay would return, but when she didn't, they made the decision to call the police. The officers, already familiar with Maymay's situation, asked KJ where he wanted to go, and to our amazement, he said he wanted to come live with us.

When the officer shared KJ's wish with us, he broke down in tears. Layla gathered him in her arms, and the officer explained that if we were not able to keep him, he would have to be placed in foster care. We assured him that wouldn't be necessary and that we would be more than happy to welcome KJ into our home. After the officer left, we did our best to comfort KJ. He cried so long that he eventually fell asleep, utterly exhausted. It felt like everything he had gone through finally overwhelmed him. As we laid him down, he whimpered throughout the night, and it broke my heart to witness such sorrow in a child. It was evident he hadn't had a peaceful night's sleep in far too long.

The next morning, when KJ woke up, the tears started again as he seemed confused and unfamiliar with his new surroundings. I walked into the room, and my presence seemed to bring him some comfort. When I picked him up, I noticed he had wet himself and felt embarrassed. Without wasting a moment, I quickly got him some clean clothes and ran a warm bath for him. It was truly incredible to witness the transformation as we tackled the layers of dirt that had accumulated; it felt like he hadn't bathed in ages. After a refreshing bubble bath, Layla whipped up a warm, inviting breakfast that filled the air with delicious aromas. While KJ found it tricky to manage his food, with more landing on the floor than in his mouth, we embraced this as a fantastic opportunity for growth that we were excited to navigate together.

Every little milestone with KJ filled our hearts with hope, love, and resilience, and I felt genuinely optimistic about the joyful journey ahead. Together, we were determined to create a nurturing environment where he could truly thrive.

One of the more significant challenges we faced was helping him adjust to breakfast in the mornings. Just the sight of food first thing made him a bit uneasy, leading to a playful mess on his plate. As this continued, it became clear that we were up against a unique hurdle, one that would inspire our creativity as we sought a delightful solution.

After some thought, we decided to try a different approach: skipping breakfast altogether. That first morning, when he woke up and found no food waiting for him, a huge smile broke across his face. It was such a relief for him to know he wouldn't feel sick. By around ten o'clock, I noticed he was getting a bit hungrier, and while I felt eager to give him something, Layla and I had our plan in mind. We understood how crucial breakfast is for a child compared to lunch, and we wanted to stick to our approach. By lunchtime, KJ was pleading for something to eat, and though we contemplated waiting until dinner, Layla couldn't resist those beautiful brown eyes, so she whipped up a classic peanut butter and jelly sandwich. He devoured it as if he hadn't eaten in days. However, when dinner rolled around, he pushed the food away, scattering it across the table and floor.

The following day, we stayed strong with our plan: a sandwich for lunch followed by a proper dinner. Gradually, we noticed the food didn't end up on the floor or table anymore. One bright morning, KJ woke Layla up, expressing his hunger. While I was still snoozing, she got up and surprised him with a plate of beignets and a tall glass of chocolate milk. From that moment on, breakfast transformed for him, he became a champion morning eater. It was so heartwarming to see him settling into this new chapter of his life.

It had been quite a while since a child had filled our home, and the memories were sweet. I reminisced about our daughter at KJ's age, her little footsteps pattering around in the early morning light. She would announce her presence with small, quick steps that grew faster as she raced towards our bedroom, bursting in with all her youthful energy. Now, it was KJ out there, trying to figure out how to join us for the day.

Since KJ came to us with nothing more than the clothes on his back, we decided to take him shopping at least once a week. The first time he stepped into a big store, his eyes lit up with wonder. He excitedly told Layla how he had never experienced shopping in such a big place filled with lights and music; he was used to only small corner stores with his mother.

One of KJ's favorite outfits was a denim jumpsuit, and I remember those evenings fondly when "The Six Million Dollar Man" was on TV. Every night at six o'clock, he could be found in front of the screen, jumping and imitating the show, completely caught up in the action. That jumpsuit became his superhero costume, and he insisted on wearing it while watching. His excitement was contagious, but as time went on, the jumpsuit became snug. Despite becoming a bit uncomfortable, he still wore it proudly, and it brought him so much joy,

Layla once tried to toss the jumpsuit, but KJ retrieved it every single time, it became a special part of him, something he held onto tightly, even sleeping with it tucked under his pillow. But then, out of the blue, he came to Layla one day and asked her to throw it away.

> I'm a big boy now, and big boys don't sleep with clothes.

His maturity in that moment was both a surprise and a delight, and it warmed her heart to see him growing up. She carefully folded the jumpsuit and stored it away with other treasured Alicentos.

When Maymay was finally released from jail, she went to live with some friends. After about a year, she returned to get KJ. We desperately wanted to keep him with us, knowing how much he had flourished in our home, but we understood he belonged with his mother. We tried our hardest to convince her to let him stay until she found a more stable place, but she interpreted our intentions differently and accused us of trying to take her child away. No matter how we tried to reassure her, her mind was made up.

As we packed his clothes into the car, I could see the mix of emotions on KJ's face. When he stepped out of the car and saw Maymay, a joyful smile spread across his face. It was clear he still loved her deeply, despite everything. He ran to her with open arms, hugging her tightly, while we drove away, and not once did he look back. It stung a bit, knowing all we had done for him, and yet he didn't say goodbye. But my heart reminded me that he was just a child, and children have an incredible capacity to love their parents, no matter what. Although this chapter with KJ may have closed, the memories we created together will always stay with us, reminding us of the beautiful experiences of family and connection.

Staying connected with KJ was a bit of a challenge, but we put in the effort because we truly cared. After a whirlwind of moving from one friend's house to another, about four to six times, she finally settled into her own apartment. This news brought us so much joy. It felt like a significant step for KJ, as she finally had a space to call home, and we were hopeful it would be a happy one. When she invited us over for dinner, her voice over the phone radiated a sense of sobriety and contentment. Perhaps time had worked some magic for her.

However, when we arrived, the scene was quite different than we imagined. While we were delighted for her new beginning, the apartment told another story. Clothes were scattered everywhere, dirty dishes filled the sink, and remnants of food and trash lay about. For a moment, we contemplated leaving, as it was overwhelming, but then we saw KJ's face, and we couldn't abandon him. Maymay looked surprised to see us, almost as if she hadn't truly expected our visit.

Layla and I shared a glance, a mix of disbelief and concern. We wanted to make the best of it, hoping to find a ray of positivity in the chaos. Unfortunately, within just an hour, Maymay became overwhelmed and started yelling at us to leave. Her words were a torrent of obscenity, and despite our attempts to calm her down, the situation spiraled further out of control. It was heart-wrenching, and we worried deeply for KJ. We asked if her son could come with us, but she vehemently insisted he stay.

In that moment, I felt a deep sorrow for him, knowing he just wanted to feel safe and loved. As we left, his mother reluctantly let him go, but it was clear he didn't want to leave her side. Standing outside the car, his big brown eyes were filled with conflicting emotions, while we could hear Maymay screaming for him to leave. My heart broke seeing him get into the car, head downcast, no doubt processing the hurtful words being shouted at him.

As we drove home, Layla turned to KJ in the backseat and then quickly faced me with tears welling in her eyes. It was a silent moment of understanding between us; we both knew the pain he was experiencing. Over the next couple of weeks, KJ stayed with us. He seemed to settle in, yet the moment he began to feel at home again, his mother demanded his return. It was heartbreaking to see him struggle with this decision, and when he told her he didn't want to return, I could see the disappointment and sadness wash over her face.

Don't worry, baby, you can come back tomorrow,

she replied, hoping to ease his mind.

After that challenging moment, we lost touch with KJ for about six months. Just before Christmas, we decided to drop off some gifts for him, filled with hope and the desire to reconnect. However, when we entered their home, our hearts sank. KJ's bed and belongings were gone, and the atmosphere felt heavy with sorrow and distress. We tried to understand what was happening, but every question met with her growing anger discouraged us from asking more.

Determined to help, Layla and I went out to buy essential items for KJ and arranged for them to be delivered. We hoped that even the smallest gestures would make a difference. Sadly, we never received a call to confirm they had reached him. The next time we saw KJ was just before we were about to leave the area. Despite all the challenges, we hold onto hope for him.

Chapter Twelve

Layla and I decided to spend our last day in the area with KJ. We drove over to his house and picked him up. As we were driving, he stared out of the back window of the moving car and whispered,

how can a little boy be expected to raise his mother?

Those were the saddest words I'd ever heard coming from a child. They were said with so much passion and understanding. My heart dropped to my stomach because I knew there was nothing, I could say to make him feel better. While staring at the back of his head, my mind drifted back to earlier times in his life. When KJ was a baby, he was the sparkle of love in his parent's eyes, and that sparkle was evident anytime you looked into his jolly little face. The more people KJ had around him the happier he seemed. It was a pleasure babysitting him because when his parents dropped him off, he seemed just as happy to be with you as you were to be with him.

At six months old, KJ's body was covered with baby fat. His cheeks were so enormous you couldn't help but rub and kiss them. When he saw your hands coming toward his face, he chuckled. His chuckles were a high pitch tone, which made you laugh along with him. As your hands moved to his face, he waved his arms and kicked his feet because he knew he was about to receive hugs and kisses and tickles under his chunky chin. He loved the attention.

As we drove down the street, KJ turned around and sat there with his little arms folded against his little chest, like a stiff board, not moving a muscle. I wondered what was going through his mind, though it was obvious that his family situation had gotten the best of him. I watched him stare straight ahead, as if he was searching for something to hold on to. As his head slowly turned in my direction, I could see tracks of tears running down his face. When he noticed I was watching, he swiftly turned his head to avoid eye contact. From his reflection in the side window, I could see his face twisting from him trying hard to stop the tears. Eventually, the emotion became too great because his face relaxed, and the tears now rushed down his precious little cheeks. As we drove, Layla glanced over at him and began to cry too. She was agonizing over what was about to happen. He never saw the tears welling in her eyes. This was a sad occasion for all of us because we were moving out of the area, one hundred miles away, and Layla knew she wouldn't be there for him.

Her motherly instincts told her not to leave him behind, but taking him with us was not an option, so she had no choice but to leave him in the unhealthy environment in which he lived.

When the car came to a red light, Layla turned and looked at the little six-year-old and wondered what would happen to him, how would he survive. He focused without blinking and stared into her eyes, she could see the pain and fears he was experiencing. When their eyes made contact, he blinked, and his eyes seemed to move in slow motion. As the car rolled down the street, he slowly turned his head and stared out of the window at a group of children playing and laughing on the side walk. We could almost see the envy he was feeling. It was as if he was saying, why I am not happy like them, or what did I do to deserve this life? Layla tried comforting him by saying we would be a phone call away, but she knew that wasn't enough. That day we did all we could to make it memorable, a day he would never forget.

We began by taking him to his favorite restaurant, McDonalds, for breakfast. He loved this place because there were always plenty of children running around, and lots of things to do while the food was being prepared. After the orders were placed, he ran out back to play on the jungle gym. He was running, jumping and climbing on everything. When he spotted the sliding board, he stopped in his tracks. This was a newly built slide that stood about twelve feet, encircled by five feet of sand. KJ slowly walked up the ladder, when he got to the top, he glanced at us to make sure we were watching. As he slid down the sliding board, the joy and excitement were evident by the gigantic smile that covered his face and the squeal that erupted from his mouth. As his speed picked up, we could see the smile being replaced by fear. When he got to the bottom, he jumped to his feet and ran over to do it again. Every so often, he yelled out for us to see what he was doing. At one point, the boy was hanging from the monkey bars swinging wildly, laughing the entire time. It was nice to see his sadness replaced by happiness, even if only temporary.

After enjoying some time on his own at the playground, KJ's day got even brighter when an old friend named Lamont, affectionately known as Monty, made his way onto the scene. As soon as KJ spotted Monty, a wave of joy swept over him, and he couldn't wait to dash over. Their reunion was filled with smiles and pure excitement. KJ quickly headed for the slide, climbing up the ladder with enthusiasm, though it was evident that Monty felt a hint of apprehension about joining in on the fun.

KJ, ever the encouraging friend, zoomed down the slide several times, his laughter ringing out like music in the air. He patiently waited for Monty to gather his courage. As Monty finally began to climb the ladder, you could see KJ cheering him on, exuding positive energy and support. Reaching the top, Monty hesitated for a moment, freezing in place. With a playful spirit, KJ stepped in front of him, joyfully sliding down with his arms flailing, laughter spilling forth. This display of reassurance seemed to inspire Monty, who slowly sat down and, with a deep breath and closed eyes, took the plunge down the slide. When he landed, his face lit up with exhilaration, and he couldn't wait to go again. Before long, both boys were gleefully sliding down with their arms in the air, sharing joyous shouts of delight.

When it was time for food, we could tell KJ was having such a fantastic time with Monty that he didn't want to pause for a meal. Each time we called him, his response was a bright-eyed, "Just one more minute, please, I'll be right there, " It was clear he was relishing every moment of their fun, so we patiently waited for him to join us. After about fifteen minutes, KJ came running in, a big smile plastered on his face and sweat glistening on his brow from all the excitement. It took him a few moments to catch his breath before he finally sat down to eat. By the time he did, his food had cooled a bit, and we wondered if he'd be willing to eat, given his somewhat picky palate. The oil from the eggs had settled on top, and the butter sat melted on his pancakes, but undeterred, KJ approached his meal with gusto, devouring it like it was the most delicious dish he had ever ate.

Once he finished, KJ spotted Monty back in the play area and immediately felt the urge to join him, though a flicker of uncertainty crossed his face about whether he could sneak in another play session. With those beautiful brown eyes glimmering with hope, he didn't have to say a thing; we understood his desire. Almost instinctively, before Layla could even give her approval, KJ sprang up and dashed off to join Monty, prompting Layla and me to exchange knowing smiles. We both chuckled, realizing that his charm was simply irresistible. Throughout the afternoon, KJ checked back to see if we were ready to leave, but he was so captivated by his play that he kept darting back for just a bit longer. After an hour of energetic fun, he slid back into his seat and declared he was ready to go, a hint of satisfaction on his face.

As we made our way to the car, KJ buzzed with curiosity about our next destination. Layla teased him with the suspense of a surprise, sparking his anticipation. I had my doubts about keeping the surprise, but as soon as we buckled him into his car seat, he succumbed to sleep. There's something incredibly precious about a child peacefully dreaming, and KJ's serene expression held a sense of complete calmness. However, once the car rolled into the mall parking lot, his eyes opened wide, taking in the surroundings with eager curiosity. He was a little puzzled, searching for familiar sights as he peered out the window, swinging his head from side to side in anticipation of the big reveal.

Approaching the entrance, we could feel his excitement bubbling up as he clutched my hand tighter, still trying to decipher our surprise destination. When we crossed through the mall doors, his face broke into a radiant smile that could light up any room; it was one of those heartwarming moments one never forgets. This mall was my favorite—not only because of its vibrant atmosphere but also because it buzzed with laughter and energy from families and children, unlike others that seemed to cater more to older crowds. It was one of the grandest shopping hubs in the area, perfect for an adventure.

As we wandered through the mall, KJ was mesmerized by the bustling sights and festive displays. The highlight was definitely the window of the Unique Gift Shop, where a little train made its joyful journey around and over the displays, captivating not just KJ but everyone who passed by. Once inside, we were greeted with even more magical moments, train stations peppered across the store, with the cheerful train whistling as passengers hopped on and off. Standing in the middle of the store, KJ's eyes followed the train in a trance-like wonder, and I couldn't help but wonder what dreams flickered through his mind. Was he imagining his own adventures on that train, exploring new lands away from home? That thought tugged at my heartstrings, but seeing his unbridled joy and excitement reminded me of the beauty of childhood moments. It was clear he was fully immersed in the experience, embracing every delightful second as if it were his first taste of pure happiness.

Leaving the gift shop, we excitedly ventured into a cheerful children's clothing store that featured a tent bursting with colorful balls at its heart. The moment KJ caught sight of that enchanting tent, his face illuminated with pure joy, sparkling like the stars in the night sky. Without hesitating, he let go of my hand and dashed over, joyfully jumping and tossing the balls into the air. While he immersed himself in play, Layla and I browsed through adorable outfits for him to try on. When we returned to the tent, my heart raced when I noticed he had disappeared, Panic set in as we called his name, anxiously searching every nook and cranny, but just then, he erupted from beneath the balls, laughter bubbling out in delightful waves. Layla's eyes shimmered with emotion; witnessing KJ's unbridled happiness was simply heartwarming.

When KJ spotted the outfits, Layla had carefully selected, he bounded out of the tent, bubbling with excitement. Each time he slipped into a new outfit, he transformed into a little model, strutting around with the kind of confidence you'd see on a fashion runway, complete with dramatic turns and expressions that could make anyone chuckle. After we bought a couple of outfits, we moved on to the next store. It was a continuation of his modeling showcase, and it was amusing to watch, even as we felt a bit wearied by the end of it. Nevertheless, KJ's energy seemed limitless, and he showed no signs of slowing down. Once we finished shopping and had all his new outfits, it was time to head back to the car.

Given all the excitement KJ had exhibited in the stores, I anticipated he would run alongside the car with the same enthusiasm. However, as soon as we hit the road, it was as if a light switch had flipped, he fell fast asleep the moment his seatbelt clicked into place. He remained in dreamland for the entire drive, upon reaching our next stop, he blinked awake and seemed to take a moment to adjust. As he surveyed his surroundings, recognition dawned, and he realized we were at the movies. A wave of exhilaration washed over him, and he burst out,

> What are we going to see? Please tell me, what are we going to see?

It was hard not to smile at his eager anticipation

When we arrived at the ticket window, KJ's eyes flitted across the colorful movie posters, trying to guess what was in store for him. The moment he spotted the film, his face lit up like a Christmas tree, grabbing my hand, he practically pulled me towards the entrance, a ball of excitement. We took a quick detour to grab some popcorn and candy before making our way into the theater, which was already bustling with kids, all buzzing with anticipation for the movie to start. As the lights dimmed and the film began, a hush fell over the theater; KJ sat mesmerized, sometimes giggling at the antics on screen like all the other kids. When the credits rolled, the theater erupted into joyful noise, but KJ remained seated, a pensive look on his face. Concerned, I asked what was on his mind. Instead of responding, he took my hand and led me out of the theater, a hint of sadness lingering in his expression that puzzled me, especially since we aimed to make the day unforgettable for him.

Upon getting back into the car, KJ surprisingly didn't drift off again. Instead, he sat quietly, reminiscent of how he had started the day, lost in thought. But as we arrived at City Park, his eyes sparkled once more. It was a beautiful day, the sun shining brightly, perfect for park adventures. KJ raced off, laughing and playing joyfully in his own world. I chased after him, and his infectious laughter rang out, so genuine that he eventually tumbled to the ground with glee, clutching his stomach as if it hurt from all the laughter. It was pure bliss to see him so carefree, reminding me of the beauty of these simple moments.

Layla lay comfortably on a blanket, soaking in the sun's gentle warmth on her face, fully appreciating this precious moment. It was tinged with bittersweetness, knowing that soon KJ would have to return to a life that was far from kind. As the afternoon faded, he stole a glance at Layla; her expression hinted at the inevitable. He sprinted over, enveloped her in his arms, and tears began to flow. With all her strength, she held KJ tightly, rocking him as if trying to erase the pain that words could never touch. They sat there together, both immersed in their shared sorrow. KJ pleaded with her, begging not to go home. Layla looked to me, her tears cascading down her cheeks, silently seeking hope. In that moment, I felt the weight of despair; there seemed to be no solution to change the reality he faced.

When we arrived at his home, Maymay was waiting on the porch, and we dropped KJ off at the entrance. The exchange of glances between him and Layla was haunting, a mix of love and deep sadness that I still carry with me. I longed to call him back, to urge him to stay with us, but I knew that wouldn't help. As we drove away, I watched him shrink in the distance, wondering what the future held for him without our support. We had been a crucial part of his world; without us, who would nurture his dreams and aspirations? The mile-long drive home felt like a lifetime, and every traffic light we encountered turned red, prolonging our anticipation. During that car ride, silence enveloped us as we were both overwhelmed by emotions.

Even more challenging than the sadness was the guilt that weighed heavily on my heart. I tried to convince myself that we had done our best, but it still broke my heart to think of a six-year-old boy navigating such a difficult situation alone. I wanted so much to suggest we stay nearby for his sake, but I knew that moving was an incredible opportunity for both of us, and deep down, I believed it was the right choice. Life had shown me that when confronted with a pivotal decision, it's crucial to choose wisely since it shapes your future. So, just two days later, we embarked on a journey toward a promising new chapter, even though it was emotionally taxing to leave KJ behind.

After we settled into our new home, a call from Maymay brightened our spirits. She asked if KJ could come to stay with us, and I remember her words vividly. She expressed her struggle in caring for him and welcomed the idea of him living with us. Our hearts swelled with joy at the thought of KJ moving in; we knew it would offer him an invaluable chance at a normal childhood. We eagerly transformed a bedroom into a welcoming space just for him, filled with love and warmth. We held our breath, waiting for that call confirming he was on his way, but instead, the call never came. While we received a couple more calls in the following days, they eventually stopped, leaving us with unanswered questions and a longing in our hearts for KJ's well-being.

Chapter Thirteen

Just a year after we settled into our new home, we received a heartbreaking call that changed everything. I vividly remember the early days of our move, when Layla and I discussed Maymay's struggles and contemplated how we might support her. Layla suggested we could help her enroll in a rehab program, but we knew that would require Maymay's willingness, and unfortunately, she seemed resistant to any advice we offered. We even considered inviting her to start fresh with us, but deep down, we recognized that unless she was ready to change, it wouldn't make any difference. It felt so disheartening, realizing our only option was to be there for her when she chose to reach out. We kept hoping and praying for her to find her path. So, when that call came, it felt like our worst fears had materialized.

I was at the hardware store picking up a ladder when suddenly, a sharp pain shot through my chest, robbing me of my breath. For a moment, panic gripped me as I thought I might be having a heart attack. I sat down on the floor, resting my head on my knees, and heard a kind voice ask,

Sir, are you alright?

After a deep breath revealed no lingering pain, I got up, feeling relieved but realizing it had been quite some time since my last checkup. Before I got home, I made a mental note to ask Layla about scheduling an appointment for me.

As I walked through the door, I noticed Layla on the phone, but it wasn't until I overheard her say, no, please tell me it isn't true, that a knot formed in my stomach. Something dreadful felt imminent, and I desperately needed to hear it from her. I watched her expressions shift, my mind swirling with dread.

Layla, what is it? What's wrong?

I couldn't contain my anxiety. For a moment, she seemed lost in thought, repeating, no, tell me it isn't true. Once she hung up, she took a seat, and placed her head in her hands. I wanted to respect her space, yet my curiosity soared, eager to know what had happened. Layla looked up at me with the saddest eyes, which sent fear down my spine. I reached out again, hoping to get clarity.

Layla, tell me what's happening. Is it about Maymay?

With a heavy nod, she confirmed my worst fear. I asked her what had happened, and I could see the weight of the news pressing on her. With her voice breaking, she told me that Maymay was in a car accident. They were driving home when she lost control. KJ was hurt, but thankfully he was wearing his seatbelt. On the other hand, she wasn't, and she was thrown from the car. The police think she might have fallen asleep at the wheel because there were no skid marks. KJ is in the hospital, and they think he will be alright.

In that moment, Layla shared that it was Keith who had reached out with this tragic news, and amidst the sorrow, he also revealed that KJ was indeed his son. A small flicker of happiness crossed my face at the news of KJ's paternity, but Layla quickly caught my reaction. She asked me why was I smiling, you could clearly see the frustration on her face. I explained that KJ being Keith's son was good news in a terrible situation, but I could feel the tension rising in the room.

> Dee, did you hear me? Maymay is gone, I don't give a fuck about KJ being his son right now. This is a huge loss for us,

Her anger and hurt were palpable, and it made me realize that while I felt a glimmer of hope for KJ, it paled in comparison to the grief that we would be facing. It struck me that Maymay could have thought that our past support of Keith, meant that there was a lack of faith in her. Although we never accused her of being unfaithful, our friendship with Keith might have implied to her that we sided with him.

That realization enveloped me in sadness, leaving me wondering how to navigate this complex situation.

As the weight of it all settled in, I knew it was important for us to honor Maymay's memory and support each other in the healing process. It wouldn't be easy, but if we kept our hearts open and leaned on each other, I believed we could find a way forward together. It was a time for compassion, understanding, and remembering the good moments we shared with Maymay, helping us find solace in the midst of our sorrow.

Later that evening, I received a call from Keith that turned into a heartfelt conversation about the troubling situation surrounding KJ. Keith's journey began when the hospital reached out to him, acknowledging him as KJ's legally recognized father. In a moment filled with chaos and uncertainty following KJ's accident, he selflessly donated blood, driven by the urgency of the moment and unaware of the genetic connection he would soon discover.

When the gravity of the situation finally settled in, he approached the doctor to clarify that he wasn't KJ's biological father. To his utter shock, the doctor confirmed the opposite: he actually was. This revelation almost snatched his soul out of his body, and it made him rethink his previous conversation with Devell. If Devell's words held any truth, it meant they were brothers, a thought that brought him pain.

As Keith spoke, I could hear the realization of what he was saying wash over him: he was now a father, a lovely thought that filled him with warmth and pride for KJ. Yet, amidst this new sense of joy, he couldn't help but reflect on his past actions, particularly regarding Maymay. He remembered the painful moment when he left her, her tears streaming down her face as she desperately pleaded with him to stay. Out of frustration, he had said hurtful things, even going so far as to spit on the ground in her direction. The image of her, devastated and alone, now haunts him, filling him with deep sorrow.

He voiced a mixture of anger and confusion towards his parents for keeping such an important truth from him. It was frustrating to think they had hidden something so significant, especially with Devell being a part of the family. This family secret had cost him a precious relationship, and Keith was beginning to unravel the impact of that omission.

As he shared this heartfelt story with me, I could feel the weight of his emotions through his voice. In a moment of silence, I sensed a shift, so I checked in with him. He confided in me about the haunting image of Maymay sitting alone, a memory that lingered painfully in his mind. I sincerely wished I could provide him with comfort or help mend the past in any way. I could sense his emotions were bubbling close to the surface, and he mentioned needing to end our call, promising to reach out later.

After we hung up, Layla entered the room, immediately sensing my unease. When I opened up about Keith's struggles, her reaction was a mixture of surprise and detachment. We had invested so much love and support into Maymay, yet it became evident that we hadn't fully grasped what Keith was experiencing. Though Maymay had worked tirelessly to hold her family together, Keith's choices had unwittingly added to her burden. This realization served as a valuable reminder of the importance of empathy, urging us to embrace each other's perspectives as caring friends.

I wanted to comfort Layla, but her perspective was undeniably valid. Seeing her in tears ignited a deep sense of resolve within me. I wrapped my arms around her, pulling her close while she rested her head against my chest. In that moment, I truly felt her sorrow and recognized my role as her pillar of strength. As the night wore on, she cried intermittently, a raw outpouring of emotion that called for patience and understanding.

The following morning, I woke up eager to lift her spirits. I decided to surprise her with a warm breakfast delivered right to the room. She gratefully appreciated the gesture, and as we shared a moment over the meal, fond memories of Maymay began to surface. While her smile was tinged with sadness, it was heartening to witness glimpses of joy, even amidst the grief. Before long, she found peace and drifted into a deep, restful sleep.

While cleaning up in the kitchen, the phone rang, and it was Keith. I expressed my concern for Layla, sharing how deeply she was feeling the loss of her friend, and even admitted that I was grappling with it too.

Keith asked if we could talk, and he began to pour out the haunting thoughts of Maymay that consumed him. He reflected on the early days of their relationship, filled with love and optimism, but with a heavy heart, he confessed his overwhelming guilt, knowing as though his past hurtful actions had contributed to her tragic fate.

His words struck a familiar chord, and as I listened, I realized the weight of his confession was becoming too heavy for me. Those brutal memories of the past surged to the forefront of my mind. Just as I was about to end the call, Keith expressed his love for me like a brother, thanking me for being there to listen. He expressed understanding if I felt the need to step back, and then he hung up.

Alone in the kitchen, I sat in contemplation about Layla and Keith, feeling a profound responsibility to support them both. I was determined not to repeat past mistakes and to truly stand by them during this challenging time. I believed deeply in the power of friendship and the importance of being there for one another, ready to navigate the road ahead with sincerity, hope, and compassion.

.

Hidden Emotions

Chapter Fourteen

Layla found herself grappling with the heartbreaking loss of Maymay, who had always been more like a sister to her. The suddenness of Maymay's passing left a heavy weight in Layla's heart. There were moments when she could smile while reminiscing about their happy memories, but then waves of grief, and anger would wash over her as she thought of the loneliness Maymay must have experienced, and the hatred she felt from Keith. It was difficult for her to find her footing in this tumultuous emotional landscape, and I could see that attending the funeral felt like an immense challenge.

We made our way to New Orleans a couple of days before the service, eager to reconnect with old friends. It was wonderful to see familiar faces, and as we shared stories from our youthful days filled with laughter and adventure, a sense of warmth enveloped us. Life may have changed with the responsibilities that come with marriage and parenthood, but those cherished memories remained vivid. Everyone knew about Maymay's struggles, yet she had been fiercely independent, often declining help. After the devastating news broke, there were whispers in the community, some believed it was a suicide, while others thought it was an accident.

On the eve of the funeral, Devell arrived clearly shaken. We were deep in conversation about Maymay when there was a knock on the door. It was Keith, and as soon as he recognized Devell, tears filled his eyes. In that moment, the truth settled over them like a warm embrace: they were brothers. Keith stepped forward and pulled Devell into a heartfelt hug, remorse spilling from him as he apologized. Here they were, facing the reality of their connection, and Keith was confronting the reality that KJ was his son, and also that Devell was his brother. During his marriage to Maymay, doctors had told him he couldn't father a child; it was understandable why he had doubted. As he cried, my heart ached alongside him.

Devell, however, struggled to contain his frustration. While he understood Keith's doubts from the past, he couldn't quite grasp why Keith hadn't trusted Maymay enough to hear her words. With a surge of emotion, he exclaimed,

> What kind of person are you? Don't you realize that if there was even a shred of a chance KJ was my son,

I would have rushed to their side and protected them from you.

Keith, feeling the weight of his own choices, admitted that the pressure of his infertility had impacted him far more deeply than he had ever acknowledged. He reflected on the emotional toll it had taken on his relationship with Maymay, once he noticed that KJ resembled Devell. No matter how hard he had tried, it always felt like a losing battle. Keith sobbed,

Why didn't I believe her? If only I hadn't been so foolish and irresponsible, Maymay might still be here. I hope everyone can find it in their hearts to forgive me. How can I face my son knowing I took his mother from him?

Devell reminded Keith that this wasn't just about seeking forgiveness from others, but rather about reconciling with himself and his faith.

You were fortunate to be bless with a wonderful partner and a child when the doctors told you it couldn't happen, and the way you showed your thanks, was to destroy your gift. You turned a vibrant woman into someone filled with anger and hurt. For heaven's sake, how could you treat her like that? She deserved so much more,

As Devell's intensity filled the space, I felt compelled to speak up.

Hold on a second, Devell, you haven't been around for years; how can you accurately judge what Maymay was going through? You didn't see how she shut everyone out or how she reacted to those who tried to support her. You weren't there for the struggles we faced.

My voice was steady, yet it carried the urgency of our shared experience. In response, Devell pressed me,

Do you have any idea where Maymay was coming from the night of the accident?

That question struck hard, and Keith couldn't contain his fury.

You son of a bitch, what were you doing with my wife?

Your wife? What do you mean by your wife? She hadn't been your wife for quite some time. She came to me because she had nowhere else to go. You have some nerve raising your voice at me after what you did to her; I have the right to knock your teeth down your stupid ass throat, and if you don't back up it could still happen. The first time I saw her; she was unrecognizable and in no condition to know who I was. I brought her to my house, hoping to provide a caring ear.

I shared with Devell that Layla and I had really tried to connect with Maymay. We put our hearts into keeping the lines of communication open, but sadly, she responded with negativity. I think the root of her feelings towards us came from our encouragement for her to reach out to you for a blood test. When you moved away, that seemed to amplify her struggles even more. We gave it our all, and it was frustrating to see our efforts go unacknowledged. Devell noticed the concern etched on our faces and reassured us, saying, "Hey, Dee, I didn't mean to suggest that you weren't trying. During our chats, Maymay realized you were there for her, even if she couldn't accept that support then. She never voiced it, but she truly appreciated everything you did for KJ."

One day, while I was heading home, I witnessed a disturbing scene: a man was trying to force a woman into his car while she was crying and desperately trying to escape. I couldn't just walk by; I stopped to help. The man accused her of stealing money, but when I looked closer, I realized in disbelief that it was Maymay. I managed to pay him off and got her safely into my car. Strange enough, when I looked into her eyes, she didn't recognize me; she saw me merely as a kind stranger coming to her aid. I brought her back to my home, and the next morning, the light began to dawn for her. When she finally recognized me, I could see the embarrassment wash over her face. She approached me with tears glistening in her eyes, and we shared a heartfelt hug. As I held her fragile form, it felt like all her pain and frustration were softening in that embrace. I knew she needed that moment of comfort, and I held on until she felt steady again.

Our conversation blossomed from there, and she began sharing the tough experiences she had faced. Eventually, the realization of who she was conversing with hit her, and in an instant, she jumped up, expressing her anger towards me, and walked out. I wanted to invite her back, to let her know she always had a place with me, but I watched her leave, feeling helpless.

Afterwards, I would occasionally see her out and about, so I decided to gradually spend more time with her to earn her trust. It took a while, but I could see her starting to open up, well, not entirely, but enough to engage in conversations. Initially, we drifted into reminiscing about the past and happier times, as if she needed to cling to those memories. Yet, the moment I attempted to discuss her current struggles, she would become furious, and it was disheartening to witness.

Then one day, while we were sharing some laughs, she suddenly unveiled her story about how she found herself in such a challenging place. The laughter quickly turned to tears, and she began to blame herself for everything, convinced that if only she had put more effort into her marriage, things could have been different. She expressed how your actions had taken a toll on her self-love, and she was determined to change that. It was heartbreaking to hear that she felt unworthy of love and incapable of giving it to others. Was anyone aware that she was attending AA meetings?

During one of our conversations about the future, she revealed that her sole motivation for moving forward was to reunite her family. It broke my heart because I couldn't quite see that vision coming to fruition, yet she believed it wholeheartedly. In light of that, I tried to utilize that family connection to provide her with support. It was a tough journey because deep down, I wished she could love me as she loved you. But what mattered most to me was that she found her strength and happiness. My hope was that once she got her life back on track, she would recognize the bond we had and see that I could be the right one for her. Keith, believe me when I say I never intended to take her from you, it was quite clear to me that you had thrown her away.

As Devell shared his thoughts, Keith chose to remain quiet, but his initial annoyance had clearly started to dissipate. He listened with the same focus and sincerity as a child would to a parent, genuinely absorbing what was being said. After a moment of reflection, Keith opened up to Devell, acknowledging that he was ultimately responsible for his actions. Tears glimmered in his eyes as he looked around at all of us, conveying a sense of vulnerability. Standing up, he walked towards the door and stated firmly,

> "I no longer feel like I belong here. What I did to Maymay was wrong, and the reasons that led me to think that way can't excuse my actions."

Layla moved closer and asked,

> "Keith, would you be willing to share what circumstances influenced you to treat her that way? I really want to understand."

He lowered his gaze and responded earnestly,

> "I wish I could find the right words to express it all, but honestly, it's hard. I've come to understand that nothing Maymay did justified how I acted."

Layla, demanded Keith to have a seat because she had something important on her mind. She shared her belief that we shouldn't let anyone run away from their challenges, highlighting the situation Maymay was in. "Just look at what happened to her," she said thoughtfully. Then, turning to Devell, she inquired about why Maymay had distanced herself from her. They had once been inseparable best friends, and Layla held on to the hope that their bond could be rekindled. She sincerely wanted to understand why Maymay hadn't reached out. Devell replied with careful consideration,

> "Layla, she really was on her way back to you, but she felt the need to distance herself from alcohol. When she realized you were moving away, it hit her harder than you might think. On the day you dropped off KJ, she watched you leave, fearful that it might be the last time she'd ever see you. I told her that when she was ready, I'd help her reconnect with you."

This message filled Layla with a renewed sense of hope. She felt a surge of excitement knowing that Maymay was actively trying to reclaim her life. Eager to learn more, Layla asked Devell about his life after leaving the neighborhood and what he knew about Alcoholics Anonymous meetings. He took a deep breath and shared,

> "When I left the neighborhood, I was facing my own struggles. Even though Maymay treated me like a friend, my feelings for her ran deeper; I never really stopped loving her. Leaving was a difficult but necessary step for me; I knew that staying would lead me down a dark path. It was harder to sever ties than I had imagined. After I joined the Air Force and faced that challenge, I thought I could navigate my life anew, but it proved to be different this time. My nights became restless, leading me to drink to cope. I felt lost, completely untethered without friends or a home. I found some solace wandering the streets at night, wrestling with my past. One night on the bus, I met an AA representative who encouraged me to attend meetings, and I've been committed to sobriety ever since."

Layla felt a deep confusion about why Devell believed he had no one to turn to, especially when he had a family that had always stood by him. She took a moment, her concern genuine, and asked why he hadn't reached out for help.

> "Honestly, Layla, my family and I aren't as close as we once were. As I grew older, I started to realize that

179

my stepfather never showed me the same love that others in the family seemed to receive. My mother and I have our chats, and she often reassured me that he tried his best given the circumstances. But every time she said given the circumstances, it felt like a reminder that I wasn't truly his child. Don't get me wrong; he never mistreated me. I just longed for that deep paternal bond I often witnessed with my sibling and in other families. I can relate to how Maymay felt, yearning for love and coming up short; it's heartbreaking. She frequently opened up about needing her husband's affection so desperately.

I wished I could be that anchor for her. But deep down, I felt I couldn't truly meet her needs. I thought if she could see someone cared for her, it might inspire her to reclaim her life. But she didn't need me to fill that void. She wasn't the type to give up; she was determined to prove she could be the woman she aspired to be. She understood that turning her life around was crucial for her child's well-being.

Layla, sensing the urgency in the moment, turned her focus to Keith and asked if he had visited KJ in the hospital. Keith fell silent, lost in thought, gazing blankly at the wall. The silence weighed heavily in the room, so Layla couldn't hold back any longer.

She yelled,

"Keith! Your son, have you even been to see him? How's he doing? Don't you care? It feels like this whole fatherhood thing is still sinking in for you. If you hadn't acted out of selfishness, maybe all of this wouldn't feel so overwhelming. I can't believe how indifferent you've been about this whole thing!"

Though her voice carried a tone of frustration, it was rooted deeply in her concern for KJ's well-being.

I tried to calm Layla, reminding her that this wasn't the right time for blame. Yet, she firmly believed her feelings were justified. With determination radiating from her, she approached Keith and pointed a finger at him with intensity. "You bastard, how could you do this to her?" she demanded, with her emotions boiling over.

Before I could step in, she unexpectedly slapped him across the face. Instinctively, I moved to pull her away, but she fought back, releasing a torrent of her frustrations and emotions. I wanted to apologize for her outburst, but the look of hurt on Keith's face indicated that words were unnecessary.

Eventually, after managing to guide Layla to a calmer spot across the room, I noticed Keith's head hung low, tears streaming silently onto the floor. Feeling a wave of compassion, I approached him, hoping to reassure him that Layla's words came from a place of hurt.

"I meant every word! Every single word!" Layla interjected; her voice defiant but also revealing her own pain.

Seeing tensions escalate, I suggested to Layla that perhaps a breath of fresh air would do us all good. Once we stepped outside, I wrapped my arms around her. At first, she resisted, but I held her firmly, emanating comfort and security. Slowly, I felt her tension begin to dissolve, and a sense of calm enveloped us both. After a while, she began to cry softly and expressed her regret over her harsh words toward Keith, but she stated she could no longer hold them in. I reassured her that there was no need for apologies; her emotions were entirely valid, and we all understood where her anger stemmed from.

In a moment filled with pain and not knowing, I saw how essential it was for us to be there for one another, even amidst the chaos.

As we made our way back into the house, Devell asked if Layla was okay. I nodded, wishing I could convey the truth behind my gesture: she still needed support and healing. I then turned my attention to Keith, asking about KJ's condition. He responded that the doctor had assured him that KJ would be fine.

> He is my son, my flesh and blood, what have I done, God, what have I done?

He needed to pull himself together, reminding him that his son needed him now more than ever.

Keith understood the weight of his responsibility. He shared that he had been at the hospital with KJ all week, observing him as he lay there, staring blankly at the ceiling, seemingly burdened by thoughts of his mother's passing, and he felt lost, unsure of how to approach the situation with his son.

I reminded him that this moment wasn't about him; it was about the little boy who just lost his mother and needed love and support, not sadness or guilt. Although the doctor had given a positive prognosis, I knew the emotional hurdles that lay ahead would require significant effort. KJ needed his father more now than ever, so it was crucial for Keith to set aside any unresolved issues with his late wife. I worried he might struggle to do this. If he truly loved her, he would recognize that the part of her still clinging to life was calling for him now, more than ever.

Keith sat in silence, clearly overwhelmed and shut off. The weight of our words seemed almost too much for him to handle. He rubbed his forehead, squinting as if each word we spoke was a sharp reminder of his pain. Leaning forward, placing his hand over his heart, he looked as though he might collapse. I was concerned for his well-being.

Are you okay? What's going on?

I called out, my voice laced with concern. He replied yes, though his eyes revealed the turmoil within. you could see that he had so much to process. Looking into my eyes, he seemed to seek understanding.

Really, I'm trying to hold it together. It's just that the guilt is heavy. How do I cope with this guilt? Why did I leave my family? All my life, I dreamed of having that family, yet I walked away from them.

I shared, we too were grappling with guilt and deep self-reflection. We echoed the same questions. While I knew she loved KJ wholeheartedly, I also understood that one of her greatest challenges was her struggle with self-love. Without loving oneself, extending love to others becomes incredibly difficult. We had waited for her to reach out, to tell us she was fine and that everything was sorted out, but that call never came.

It's clear that we recognize her troubles, we knew that there was little we could do without her desire to seek help. That's what everyone says: if someone doesn't ask for help, there's nothing you can do. But I wondered: is that truly the case, or is it just a way for us to avoid confronting harsh realities?

Despite the challenges we faced, I felt a glimmer of hope that with love and support, healing could begin for both KJ and Keith. Together, we could work towards a brighter future.

Chapter Fifteen

On the morning of the funeral, we couldn't find Keith anywhere. It felt like a possibility that he might not come, especially since our last interaction left him seeming so distant and disconnected. The whirlwind of events from the past week were undoubtedly overwhelming for him. Despite the difficulties he had put Maymay through, I still believed he deserved a chance at redemption. I couldn't abandon another friend in need.

Layla's heart was still too heavy to forgive him, or us for that matter. She was battling with her emotions, feeling twenty percent anger towards him, while the other eighty percent was directed at us for not stepping in more decisively to support one of our closest friends. Her emotions bubbled over at times, oscillating between calm and frustration. I'll never forget that moment in the restaurant when the waitress asked us if we were ready to order, and Layla erupted, telling her to give us some time, please. I felt a wave of embarrassment wash over me, but I recognized that her outbursts were part of her grieving process. She needed the space to navigate her feelings, and it truly pained me to watch her struggle.

However, a turning point in her recovery appeared to come when we made the decision to visit Maymay and Keith's old house, the very place where their family story began and concluded. We hoped that stepping into that familiar space would help us find some clarity and connection again.

Arriving at the house, we found it empty, which felt like a blessing in disguise. It granted us the freedom to explore without the weight of distraction. As we walked through the gate towards the front door, Layla hesitated, expressing that she couldn't bring herself to go inside. I reminded her that this visit was essential for both of our journeys toward healing. I remembered how my mom sought solace in her mother's home after her passing, perhaps we could find a similar sense of peace. Taking her hand in mine, I encouraged her to come with me, and as we stepped over that threshold, a wave of warmth enveloped us. It seemed like a hint of the joy that once thrived in Maymay and Keith's family, sparking fond memories that danced in our minds. I caught Layla's gaze, and a smile blossomed on her face. When I asked what she was thinking, she reminisced about a party we had shared, and I couldn't help but return her smile, I was thinking of that same joyful moment,

As we wandered through the house, my feelings began to shift. I vividly recalled the incident when Keith had shaken KJ and dropped him on the floor. Layla gripped my hand tightly, an unspoken understanding passing between us. Suddenly, she halted, her face clouded with recognition. With every step through the house, the atmosphere thickened with memories that sometimes hurt to revisit. But when we finally opened the back door, it felt as if a breeze swept through, carrying some of the sadness away. We took a moment to sit in the backyard, reflecting on our lives and feeling grateful for the support we found in each other.

On our way back to the hotel, we decided to swing by the home of some old friends. It was a bittersweet visit, as the atmosphere was thick with their struggle to cope with the recent loss. Everyone had held onto hope, believing that she might overcome her personal battles. Our friends shared that we wouldn't have recognized her; her once vibrant hair was now tangled and disheveled, a stark contrast to the lively spirit we remembered. They recounted times when she would wander into the neighborhood, seemingly lost and confused about why she was there. Sometimes, she would crash at someone's place for a few days, only to vanish again.

This left us with many questions about KJ and his world during her absences. We couldn't help but wonder what he had witnessed and how he was managing through it all. His well-being was a constant concern.

Returning to the hotel, I noticed Layla looked utterly exhausted as she lay down. Recognizing that she needed some rest, I decided to check on Keith after she fell asleep. I meant to take a quick moment to gather my thoughts, but the next thing I knew, Devell was knocking at the door. I opened it to find him already dressed and ready to go. Surprised, I glanced at the clock and realized five hours had flown by. I called for Layla to wake up, but when I didn't hear her, I turned back and was taken aback to see her standing beside Devell, completely dressed and looking anxious. She explained that she didn't want to disturb me while I was sleeping so deeply, so she had gone out for a bit. When she returned and saw me still asleep, she got ready in hopes of waking me before leaving. When that didn't happen, she felt worried and called Devell for support.

In that moment, I was surprised by my own exhaustion; sitting on the edge of the bed, I struggled to keep my eyes open. Layla's voice was laced with concern when she asked if I was alright. I wanted to reassure her, but the words felt stuck, and I briefly feared something was wrong. When I stood up to face her and Devell, Layla asked again with genuine worry. This time I managed a response, though I didn't want to burden her with my concerns; she had enough on her plate. I made my way to the bathroom to get dressed, and as I glanced at my reflection, I acknowledged that I wasn't feeling my best. Still, I was resolved to hold it together until we got back home.

After a refreshing shower, I felt revitalized. Dressed and renewed, we set out to meet our friends at the church, where we reminisced about Maymay fondly. It was heartwarming to share stories and laughter, to keep her memory alive in our hearts. Every moment reminded us of the connections we cherish and the hope we carry moving forward.

The atmosphere at the church was truly heartwarming as everyone who knew Maymay came together. It felt like a fantastic reunion, especially since many of us hadn't seen each other since moving away from the neighborhood. As the minister began his heartfelt message, I could hear soft sobs echoing through the space, a testament to the profound sorrow and loss we were all feeling. It was clear to us all that Maymay deserved so much better than the difficult life that had come her way.

Then, an incredible moment graced us when the church fell silent. I glanced behind me and was overjoyed to see Keith holding KJ close in his arms. He made his way to the front of the church and sat right next to me. Although he didn't glance my way or utter a word, his focus was unwavering. I sensed the congregation's eyes on him, but he seemed completely composed, holding his son tightly and displaying remarkable strength. Witnessing his courage filled me with hope, if he could navigate this painful chapter, perhaps there was resilience in all of us to face whatever the future might bring.

When the minister concluded his moving sermon, he invited anyone who wished to share a few words about Maymay to come forward. The line grew long, but it was Layla who truly captured the essence of our collective feelings. As she stepped up to the podium, I noticed her knees tremble slightly. I instinctively stood, but she raised her hand, signaling that she was fine. She took a moment to gather herself, gazing over the room before speaking, then paused thoughtfully. Instead of continuing, she walked down from the podium and approached Maymay's casket. There, staring earnestly, she shared these words:

> I've known Maymay my whole life. Back when we were teenagers, we often imagined this day and joked about who would be up here speaking and who would be there. I've always felt she knew this would be my role somehow. So, here's what we decided I should say: To her beloved child, she loved you deeply. To her husband, she loved you and truly hoped to be everything you needed. To her friends, she loved you dearly and hoped she was the friend you all deserved. Finally, she wanted me to share something humorous: no more broccoli to eat, no more painful perms to sit through, no more worries, and most importantly, no more periods.

This brought soft laughter through the crowd, lightening the somber atmosphere. Layla looked at her dear friend and said,

> Alright, I said it. I hope you're smiling now that I've made a bit of a fool of myself, after all, a promise is a promise.

Turning back to the audience, her tone shifted.

On a more serious note, I miss her. I miss her more than words can express. The world has lost a truly good spirit, and with everything going on, it needs all the good spirits it can get. I've lost a wonderful friend, and those are hard to come by. KJ has lost his mother, and there's simply nothing that can replace a mother's love. Keith has lost a wife, a realization that she truly was a precious gift in his life.

Yet, she has given us a remarkable gift that we can cherish forever: KJ, her beautiful child. This reminds us to love those we hold dear while they're still with us.

After bidding farewell to Maymay, Layla returned to her seat, and I glanced over at Keith again. Tears glistened on his cheeks as he exchanged a bittersweet smile with Layla before looking straight ahead. The moment was poignant, a mixture of grief and gratitude.

After the service, we made our way back home, reflecting on KJ and Keith. What lay ahead for them? How would Keith navigate parenting KJ alone, knowing that he could have had a full life with Maymay at his side? Would he find a way to move forward or become anchored in the past? My heart ached for KJ, who would also need to come to terms with the repercussions of Keith's earlier choices.

Chapter Sixteen

Two months had passed since the funeral, and Layla finally felt ready to say Maymay's name without tears streaming down her face. It was a significant moment for her, and she shared with me that she had dreamt about Maymay being in a beautiful, peaceful place, free of any anger or sadness. In that moment, she found solace because seeing Maymay at rest reminded her of the beautiful soul she was: a truly compassionate and loving friend. It filled me with relief. This was a breakthrough because it meant we could finally have an open and honest conversation about what had taken place in New Orleans, about the house, the funeral, and Keith.

Layla recognized that walking through the house acted as a spiritual cleansing for her heart and soul, an essential step in her journey of healing. The funeral became not just a goodbye, but a celebration of Maymay's life, a chance to reflect on the love they shared.

Curiosity bubbled up within me regarding how Layla felt about Keith. To my joy, she expressed that if Maymay could forgive him, then she could too. That realization brought a smile to my face, and I felt confident that Keith would be touched to hear those words from her. He had been reaching out to her, wanting to talk, though Layla hadn't been ready to answer his calls. But after our heartfelt conversation, they finally connected.

From the kitchen, I listened as their voices intertwined, filled with laughter and a few tears, a beautiful mix of emotions. It felt promising, that perhaps this conversation would rebuild some bridges, but curiously, Keith seemed to pull back afterward and stopped calling altogether.

Every now and then, we would hear from Devell, who kept us updated on how things were going for him. Whenever we asked about Keith and KJ, Devell would say he hadn't seen them much lately. My heart ached with worry for them, wondering what they were going through.

Just as I decided it was time to go find them, Keith unexpectedly called. Coincidentally, it was exactly one year after the funeral. He wanted to know if he and KJ could come visit us. My heart leaped at the thought. We were excited for two reasons: we would get to see KJ and it was hopeful knowing they had both survived what must have been an incredibly challenging year. Keith mentioned they would be arriving in a couple of weeks, which gave us time to prepare for a joyous reunion.

The special day finally arrived, and there was a knock at the door. Layla opened it, and to our surprise, there stood KJ, looking more grown-up than ever. I couldn't believe how much he had transformed in just a year. When Layla tried to pick him up, he stood his ground, so instead, she wrapped her arms around him in a warm hug. It was a wonderful reminder that he was now eight years old, a big-hearted young boy where just yesterday it felt like he was this little bundle of energy.

It felt magical sharing this joyous moment with each other again. Seeing KJ's bright smile brought so much happiness to us; our worries about him forgetting us melted away when we realized he hadn't forgotten at all. Just as I was about to ask KJ about his dad, Keith appeared.

Layla rushed over and embraced Keith, pulling him in with a hug. He looked slightly surprised but reveled in her affection, showing no sign of discomfort. I extended my hand toward Keith, and at first, he looked a bit uncertain, but then he took hold of my hand, pulling me in for a big bear hug. In that moment, I felt a spark of the old connection we once had, as if he was starting to rediscover himself again. This reunion felt like the beginning of a new chapter for all of us, one filled with hope, love, and the promise of healing together.

As we gathered together, sharing heartfelt memories of our younger days, the adventures we embarked on and the magical places we visited. One of our absolute favorite summer hangouts was the sprawling pool at Audubon Park. We were absolutely thrilled every time we went, especially because of the iconic high diving board. As kids, that ladder felt like it led us straight to the heavens, and standing at the top made us feel like we were on top of the world, it was quite a scene to see some kids climb up only to back down when faced with the height. But those of us who found the courage to take that leap were rewarded with an exhilarating thrill, almost like flying.

One summer, the pool had to close for renovations, but it reopened just in time for its incredible 100th anniversary celebration. After that, life took over, and we didn't return for a long time. However, once we learned it was open again, we knew we had to take a nostalgic dive off that board once more. By then, we were grown-ups, and we were taken aback when we stepped out to the pool area. The high diving board we had longed for all those years turned out to be surprisingly modest, only about ten feet tall. To our adult perspective, it wasn't nearly as grand as we remembered. The lifeguard shared that many adults felt just like us, surprised by the newfound reality. To kids, that diver's platform truly felt like it touched the sky.

Despite our initial disappointment, we decided to go for it anyway. To our joy, when we reached the top, the rush of excitement felt just as exhilarating as it did back then.

We also reminisced about the fun-filled chaos of Mardi Gras, remember how thrilled we were to finally attend a parade without our parents? By the time we hit our teenage years, most kids ventured out to parades on their own. Yet, our parents loved the festivities, often joining us. We would stroll ahead of them, hoping no one would realize our connection. But somehow, by the day's end, a schoolmate would always appear, and without fail, one of our parents would say something that would earn us giggles and embarrassed reactions.

I vividly recall the first time we found out we could attend a parade solo. We were bubbling with happiness, not knowing how to contain our excitement. Even though it wasn't Mardi Gras Day yet, any of the nightly parades felt like a dream come true. Our parents asked us to come up with a plan in case we got separated, but, honestly, we didn't give it much thought. After all, nothing had gone wrong in the past, so we figured we were in the clear. We could hardly wait for 5:30 to hop on the bus to Uptown, where the parades were set to kick off at 6:00 PM.

The energy on the way was electric, laughter and playful shoving filled the air as we reveled in the moment. But it wasn't long before a sudden wave of chaos overtook the street. People began to run, and even to this day, we still can't figure out why. Instinct kicked in, and we found ourselves running right along with them. Just as quickly as it began, the commotion subsided. Suddenly, I realized I had lost sight of my friends. Anxiously, I tried to remember our agreed-upon meeting spot: the corner of Canal Street. As I made my way there, I couldn't help but wonder which cross street we had actually discussed; of course, we hadn't nailed that down at all.

Peering down Canal, I felt overwhelmed by the sheer number of people. But then, I spotted Keith looking around, full of determination. A wave of relief washed over me as I called his name, when he finally saw me, he dashed over. Just then, Devell joined us, and together, we realized we had to find the girls, we couldn't possibly go home without them.

Up and down Canal Street we went, searching high and low for any sign of our friends. Just when we were about to lose hope, something nudged us to return to the scene of the initial chaos. And there they were, beaming and lost in the parade's sights and sounds. They assured us they had figured we would eventually find our way back. They had made a pact to meet at the last spot they saw each other. What a blessing that was. That night turned into an unforgettable adventure as we explored the French Quarter and meandered down Bourbon Street, creating some of the most cherished memories ever.

.

Chapter Seventeen

The following morning brought a sense of renewed hope as Layla rose early to prepare breakfast. It was heartwarming to see KJ already seated at the table, eagerly awaiting his meal. His presence reassured us that he enjoyed a routine of sharing breakfast together, and that was a wonderful sign. As we gathered around the table, a silence enveloped us. Perhaps we had exchanged all our thoughts the night before, and our minds were still processing everything that had unfolded. Usually, we would discuss things over breakfast, but during the night I had a dream that weighed heavily on my heart, and I wasn't ready to share it, especially with Keith nearby.

After KJ finished his meal, he excitedly hopped up and bounded off to the living room to watch cartoons. A few moments later, Layla followed him, and as she left, I reassured her that we would have our conversation later. She shot me a playful evil eye, which made me smile as I winked back at her, breaking the tension with a hint of lightheartedness.

Once we were alone, I turned to Keith and noticed tears shimmering in his eyes. He seemed to be putting up a brave front, desperately trying to hold back his emotions. Concerned, I asked him if he was alright. He opened up, sharing that being with us felt comforting. I quickly reassured that what truly mattered was the bond he was building with KJ.

> Dee, I know this might sound a bit out there, but I need to talk about something that's been weighing on my mind. For a while now, I've been having the same dream repeatedly. It always begins with me and Maymay sitting at a table. She's positioned away from me, wearing a flowing silk gown that billows gently as if stirred by an invisible breeze. No matter how hard I try to see her face, she always eludes my gaze. Then, it's like we're on a carousel; the faster I try to look at her, the quicker it spins.
>
> Eventually, the carousel spins so wildly that I feel I'm about to be thrown off. As a last resort, I reach out to her, but when I grab her shoulder, the ride halts suddenly. Instead of seeing her face, I find myself lying on a table, looking up at her. The dreams conclude in the same way, I slide through her body and always hear her softly say, do the right thing. I'm

left with the quest of understanding what that means, and she always responds, that I will know when it happens. Though these dreams have haunted me night after night, last night was different; for the first time, I slept deeply, no tossing or turning. I believe I'm starting to understand something significant. We're here for a reason, and although I'm uncertain about it now, I remain hopeful that by the end of this visit, everything will become clear.

As Keith shared his experience, I felt a strong urge to confide in him about my own dream, but I held back. It felt too fresh, too overwhelming, and I realized that he had enough on his plate already. Having Maymay return and share such weighty messages must have been incredibly daunting for him. My hope was that my dream would remain a singular experience. To shift the focus, I inquired about how KJ was managing all of this.

Not too well, he hasn't muttered a word since the accident. The doctors assure me there's nothing physically wrong with him, and they believe he'll speak when he's ready. Sometimes, he just stares at me with tear-filled eyes. I can only imagine the storm of thoughts swirling in his mind. I've tried everything I could think of to encourage him to talk, but nothing seems to reach him.

Keith's words revealed a depth of concern and love for KJ, which I found truly commendable. I could sense that we were all on a journey together, and despite the challenges we faced, there was a thread of hope that connected us all.

About a month after Maymay's death, I walked pass his room and could've sworn I heard him talking to someone. I burst into the room, and he was asleep. I pulled up a chair, and sat by his side in hopes that I would hear his voice but heard nothing. Even if he was talking in his sleep, I wanted to hear something. I needed to talk to him about what happened to his mother, and how he felt about me. Sometimes he looks at me with so much anger; it seems as if he would rip my head off if he could. Other times the expression on KJ's face says he needs to be held, but when I walk toward him, he turns away. During those times, I can't explain the pain I feel when I can't comfort him. I wonder what he knows. What did he remember about me and his mother's relationship? How does he feel about me? Most of his life I've been a jerk or worse, the one who ruined his family, the one who caused his mother to reject him, the one who may have caused his mother's death. What can I do to make any of this up to him? How can I ever make this right?

It's been a year, and he hasn't opened up to me yet. Maybe I'm the problem; maybe seeing me day in and day out makes him sick. Maybe my face reminds him of what happened to his mother.

Dee interrupted him,

Look, the only thing I can say is talk to your son. Even if he doesn't talk back let him know your thoughts. You are the adult, his father, and you might have to make up for some of your indiscretions. Show him that you love him, and you'll be there for him. He's been through a lot.

Maybe I'm supposed to leave him here with you and Layla, that's what Maymay is trying to tell me. She doesn't want my son... I mean her son to be with me.

No, you were right the first time. He's your son, and I don't believe she would want you to leave him here, not that we wouldn't love to have him. He's a loving child, but he should be with his father. If you don't think you can handle him and give him the love he needs, then sure, you can leave him here. Do you love KJ?

Of course I do, more than life itself, he's my flesh and blood, my son, and I love him. I want to do the right thing, and if the right thing is to leave him, I'm willing to do that also. Like I said, by the end of the trip, I'll know what to do.

Whatever you decide we'll support you in your decision.

I have two weeks to try and figure things out, and then I'll have to get back to work.

By the way, where are you working?

When I first went back to work, I worked for Backland Enterprise. It was hard work with very little benefits. Every day we met at the office, loaded onto trucks and were dropped off at a work site. There was a crew bagging sand, another crew walking the sand bags over to us and we tossed them onto the trucks. This was back breaking work and it seemed as if there was an endless number of bags to load. Every day I had dirt covering me from head to toe. One day while I was having lunch, I felt someone staring at me. I turned around and it was Bob. I could see he was trying to figure out where he knew me from. At first, I wasn't going to say anything, but something told me to go and talk to him. When I called him by his name, he took a couple of steps back and said, do I know you? I told him it was me, Keith Jackson. He remembered me and asked how my family was doing.

I explained that Maymay had passed away, but KJ and I were doing fine. Bob seemed to be genuinely shaken by this; he asked me when it happened. I told him and he said he had seen her a few months before her death at an AA meeting. They had spoken several times and the last time he saw her; she asked him if I could get my job back. Can you believe it, after all I did to her, she had not given up on me. Bob and I sat and talked about our past working relationship, and since I no longer worked for him, there was something I always wanted to ask him. Why on the day the police stopped me in the parking lot did he react the way he did. I knew if he'd spoken to the officers when he first walked up it would've saved me a lot of bull shit time. All he had to say was, you have the wrong man. So, I wanted to know, why he didn't speak up for me. After all, I thought we were pretty good friends. He remembered the incident, and then told me the truth of why he didn't want to get involved with the officers.

One day, he was on his way to work when he first encountered the same two police officers. He said he would never forget their faces or that day. When Bob approached the officers in the parking lot, they clearly recognized him too.

It all started one morning when a young man suddenly ran into the street. he didn't see him until the young man collided with the side of his car. He slammed on his brakes, and just as he was about to exit the vehicle, the two officers came rushing around the corner, shouting for him to stay in the car and move on. The young man pleaded not to leave, insisting that the officers were going to kill him. He didn't believe him and thought the kid must have done something wrong and was just trying to escape. So, he drove off without giving it much thought.

Two days later, the young man's body was found, beaten almost beyond recognition. He wanted to convince himself it wasn't the same person, but knew it was. he considered going to the police, but understood that they were part of the problem. After the body was discovered, the officers began to follow him. After two weeks of this, they pulled him over and questioned him about what had happened. Their demeanor and the way they spoke sent chills down his spine. He explained that he hadn't seen anything, and they eventually let him go.

When he later saw the same officers with me, he felt scared. Initially, he thought about walking past as if he hadn't seen anything, but as he got closer, he noticed one officer's foot on my neck and couldn't just walk away.

After his encounter with those officers, Bob faced daily harassment from them. About a year later, the two officers were charged with the murder of that young man and six others, some murders occurred before the incident he witnessed, while others took place afterward. Bob believed that if he had spoken up in the beginning, he might have been able to save the others.

While telling his story, tears streamed down Bob's face. he knew there was nothing he could do to ease his pain. As I listened, my boss stormed in, yelling at me to get back to work before I got fired. Before I could respond, Bob said, if you need a job, your old one is waiting for you. When we heard the door slam, he remarked, I guess that means you'll take the job. I asked if I could start the following day, and he nodded in agreement.

As I was getting up to leave, Bob said, welcome back. On his way home, Keith reflected on what Bob had shared and how much he had resented him for not speaking up during his encounter with the police. It made him realize that you can't judge people solely by what you see, and, of course, it reminded him of Maymay, as he had done the same thing to her.

Hidden Emotions

Chapter Eighteen

Keith told me that his life had been spinning out of control when he met a woman, her name was Fran. She knew he was married, and having problems. He told her he thought his son was the result of an affair. She thought he was trying to make her feel he had been dishonored by his wife and that would justify her being with someone else's husband. Of course, she didn't believe him because that line was used by more men than she could count. She explained that as long as he was married, they could only be friends. He was ok with that, but as time went by Fran asked him to move in with her. When he first moved in, he felt like a new man, so he concluded that it was Maymay that was holding him back.

One day they were talking about their feelings and she told him he was still in love with his wife and should try to put his marriage back together. He didn't believe what she was saying because the only thing he felt for his wife was disgust. He insisted that he could never be with a woman who cheated. Fran wanted to know if he considered their relationship cheating. Because he was still married, but living with her. How did he think Maymay felt about that? Keith didn't have an answer, but he knew Fran was right.

Keith started concentrating on building a relationship with Fran, taking her out to dinner, going dancing, and treating her like she was the only woman in his life. He wanted her to know that he wanted to be with her, and he would divorce Maymay and marry her. He thought it was important that Fran knew he was ready to start over, and she was the one he wanted to spend the rest of his life with.

Fran told Keith she felt the same way, but she didn't want to get hurt again. She thought her marriage was perfect, her husband worked for the government making decent money. One day he came home, packed his stuff, and told her he wanted a divorce. She wouldn't have to worry about money because he would continue taking care of her and his son. That was the way her marriage ended. One day they were a loving family and the next day she was alone with her son. She had separated from her husband three years before she met Keith.

Keith wanted to know if Fran ever found out what happened to her husband and she said,

Every two weeks she received money from him. Six months after he left, he returned. He wanted to spend some time with his son. Before she agreed to let him see his son, he had to tell her what was going on in his life. He told her he was gay, actually, he said he knew it all his life, but he wanted desperately to fit in with everybody else. He realized he could no longer live the lie. He said he had three choices, cheat, kill his self, or be honest. And he hoped she could respect his decision. When he first told her, she flipped out, threw him out, and told him he should have killed himself. She thought he would stop sending her money, and she would have to take him to court, but the money continued, so it forced her to rethink her attitude toward him. She realized that she didn't wish for any harm to come to him, nor did she want to be intimate with him if he was involved with someone else. Embracing his honesty allowed her to find peace. They've become great friends; he takes their kid on some weekends, and they genuinely seem to have built a wonderful relationship together.

She often reminded me that just because I was separated, it didn't mean there was no potential for friendship with my ex-wife. I completely understood her point and was in the process of reaching out to Maymay when I received news about the accident. When I discovered that KJ was my son, both Fran and I recognized that our relationship would be challenging to sustain since it was built on the shaky foundations of Maymay's infidelity and the belief that

KJ wasn't mine. It was clear that if I wanted to move forward and get my life back on track, I needed to let go of the past.

After KJ and I settled into our new apartment, I decided to hire a babysitter for him. One evening, I came home to a heartwarming sight: Fran was at the house, gently cradling KJ, who was peacefully sleeping on the couch. The babysitter had gotten sick and reached out to Fran for help. As I moved closer to lay KJ down, I could feel the tranquility in the room. When Fran looked at me, I sensed that her feelings for me were still there. Before leaving, she expressed her love for both me and KJ, assuring me that when I was ready to love again, she would be waiting. I pondered her words deeply, attempting to sort through my feelings toward her, yet I found my heart still leaning toward Maymay. As I compared my emotions for both women throughout the night, I realized that whenever I imagined loving Fran, Maymay's image would flash in my mind, leaving me questioning whether my feelings for Fran were genuine or if I was simply not ready to embrace new love.

The next morning, when the babysitter called to say she was still unwell, I reached out to Fran once more. She kindly agreed to look after KJ, but I would need to drop him off at her place. I quickly realized that Fran had stepped up to babysit consistently throughout the week. Then I received a call from my babysitter announcing that she was pregnant and wouldn't be returning. I hesitated to ask Fran if she could take over as KJ's permanent babysitter because I understood the feelings that complicated our relationship. I couldn't imagine forging a bond without feeling like I was taking advantage of her emotions. When I shared my concerns with her, she sweetly insisted that it didn't matter; taking care of KJ would be a joy for her. This arrangement lifted a huge weight off my shoulders. As we started to rebuild our friendship, we shared delightful dinners, enjoyed movies, and participated in various fun activities together.

One day after work, as I went to pick up KJ, I noticed a man at Fran's house. When she explained that they were simply friends, I felt an unexpected surge of anger. I didn't say much; I just picked KJ up and left. As I drove home, I couldn't quite grasp why I felt so upset. I had clearly established in my mind that Fran and I were friends, so what was causing this emotional turmoil?

The next day, I reached out to my boss and asked for a day off, citing that I had some pressing personal matters to attend to. I felt a little guilty about lying, especially given that I had just started, but I needed the time to confront the whirlwind of emotions I was experiencing before they spiraled into something I couldn't control. I had learned through tough experiences how detrimental it could be to bottle up feelings. I couldn't help but think about how different things might have been with Maymay had I addressed my feelings sooner.

I decided not to call Fran to inform her that I wouldn't be bringing KJ over, and to this day, I wonder why I chose not to reach out. Ultimately, she called me, and when I told her I was off and that KJ wouldn't be coming over, I sensed that she wanted to discuss things further, but I just wasn't ready for that conversation, so I hung up. About an hour later, there was a knock at my door. I didn't answer, knowing it was her. She knocked persistently before eventually leaving. I began to wonder why I hadn't just opened the door. Something was changing within me, and I couldn't quite understand what it was. That was also when the dreams began, visions of Maymay as if she were trying to communicate something to me.

The following morning, I dropped KJ off without saying a word to Fran. I could tell she felt hurt by my actions, and I found myself at a loss for how to remedy the situation.

Over time, I started to realize just how meaningful my friendship with her was, especially when I noticed a man frequently coming and going from her house. It hit me hard, I felt like I had lost a good friend. So, I mustered the courage to tell her just how much I missed the bond we shared. To my surprise, she responded with warmth, assuring me that our friendship was very much alive and that it was on me to reach out and reconnect. Her words brought tears to my eyes, I walked over, gave her a heartfelt hug, and told her she was a true friend. I expressed my sincere apologies for acting as if our friendship didn't matter. It was a beautiful moment that reaffirmed our connection,

After a month on the job, I received the exciting news that I was being promoted back to my old department, As I pulled into the parking lot, a rush of emotions washed over me, what an incredible twist of fate. I sat in the car, feeling slightly overwhelmed and a bit nervous about how everyone would perceive my return, especially after everything I had been through. Just then, I had a surprise visitor, Bob knocked on my window. I hadn't even seen him approach, and it startled me. His friendly concern shone through as he asked if I was okay. For a moment, I could only see his lips moving, but he repeated his question, making it clear he truly cared.

I opened the door and stepped out, grateful for his support. As we walked toward the building, I felt my nerves kick in, and my knees started to tremble. I paused and placed my hand on his shoulder for a moment; he looked at me with understanding but didn't say a word as we continued our walk. Once we entered the building, I felt a surge of confidence, and my legs regained their strength. After handling the paperwork at Human Resources, Bob guided me to my desk, and I was overjoyed to find it was the same one I had before. Even though most of my coworkers were new faces who had joined after my absence, their fresh energy helped me ease back into my routine.

Yet, every time the phone rang, my heart raced like never before. I soon realized why: I was subconsciously waiting for Maymay's familiar voice. It brought back memories of how she would call me every morning without fail, pouring out her love and counting down the moments until my return home. In those precious moments, I hadn't comprehended just how supportive she was, or how radiant her beautiful smile could be. My heart ached to see that smile one more time. Why did it take her passing for me to recognize such a profound truth?

As we sat at the kitchen table reflecting, Layla brightened the entrance with a cheerful good morning I couldn't resist responding, actually, it's more of a good evening. She asked for the time, and I reminded her that she had taken a nap, and it was the afternoon. Curiously, Keith inquired about KJ's whereabouts, and Layla's alarmed reaction was instant, she exclaimed, where could he be?

As we stepped into the living room, we quickly realized that the front door was wide open. Panic set in as Keith dashed outside, calling out for KJ with a sense of urgency. In that moment, I could see fear flicker in his eyes, a haunting recognition that, because KJ hadn't spoken since the death of his mother, he might not get an answer. It felt like a scene pulled straight from a nightmare, one that none of us wanted to face.

Keith then shared a dream he had experienced just the night before. In it, he and KJ were having the most wonderful father-son day at the mall, filled with smiles and laughter. But suddenly, panic gripped him when he looked down and saw that the child holding his hand wasn't KJ. Instead, the terrified little one jerked away, sprinting back to his mother, who, in a frantic state, began shouting for the police, convinced that Keith was a stranger trying to take her child. It was a surreal and confusing moment for him, caught up in what felt like an alternate reality.

Reflecting on what had happened in the last few minutes, Keith remembered his joyful time at the toy store, where he made a quick trip to the restroom, and upon returning, he merely grabbed what he thought was KJ's hand and left without confirming it was really his son. Once he convinced the officer of the mistake, he began walking through the searching for KJ.

Approaching another police officer, he explained that he had lost KJ and shared his son's age and name. But at that instant, the harrowing truth struck him: no matter how loudly he shouted, KJ couldn't answer.

Then, in a hopeful turn, the officer used a loudspeaker to call out for KJ. Keith's heart raced as he saw a small boy moving toward him. He picked up speed, only to realize the child wasn't KJ. Desperation flooded him again, and he called out KJ's name with everything he had. And suddenly, from the distance, a sweet voice burst through the air: "Daddy, I'm here, over here,"

His heart soared as he dashed toward the sound, yet the more he ran, the farther the voice seemed. Glancing up at the second floor, he saw a man with KJ, pulling him away. In a frenzy, he searched for a way upstairs but found none. With determination, he jumped, trying to reach that elusive floor, waking up in a panic.

Back in the real world, Keith and I were in the backyard when Layla stepped outside with a sparkle in her eye, announcing, he's here. To our immense relief, it turned out KJ had simply grown tired and decided to go back to bed. The moment Keith caught sight of him, relief washed over him, and he scooped KJ into a tight embrace, holding him as close as humanly possible.

KJ was quiet though, not even wrapping his arms around his dad in the usual playful manner. He looked stiff and still, and I could see the sadness in Keith's eyes, echoing a moment from the past when KJ had looked up at us with the same expression after we'd dropped him off from a fun park day. Stealing a glance at Layla, I noticed tears brimming in her eyes.

Chapter Nineteen

fter we found KJ, we all gathered in the living room, and it instantly became clear that Layla was feeling quite upset. Keith noticed her distress and immediately asked what was wrong, but she didn't reply. Instead, she took KJ's hand and headed to the bedroom. I considered telling him the truth about Layla's feelings, but I didn't want to add to the tension. So, I simply said that it was tough for her to see KJ feeling so distant from everyone.

Keith was eager to comfort his son, but every time he attempted to approach him, he would become stand off-ish. He confided in me that he had tried everything to bridge the gap with KJ, but nothing seemed effective. He held onto hope that maybe our presence might help KJ break free from his emotional numbness. Keith believed that if KJ could express his feelings, it would open the door to a conversation between them, because he hadn't spoken a word since his mother's death.

In the meantime, KJ sat quietly in his room, absorbing everything we were saying. Despite his silence, I knew he was processing it all.

In his thoughts, KJ reflected,

> *There's nothing you could do to change how I feel about you, nothing at all. I remember so much from the past. I remember you telling my mother I wasn't your son, and at that time, I didn't quite grasp it, but over the years, you made sure I understood exactly what that meant. You spoke so harshly about her that I almost thought whore was part of her name. You really don't want me to talk to you; you don't want to know how I feel.*

I suggested that opening up to his son about his own struggles might help KJ relate to him better. Keith insisted he had made every effort and wondered how he could explain to a child that his father was an awful person, that no one should have to endure the hardships they went through. While it feels overwhelming, he must find a way to bridge that gap.

As KJ contemplated his feelings, he thought,

> *You should feel embarrassed, humiliated, and disgusted. I remember waking up in the middle of*

the night to find you and her standing there, your hand at the back of her head, pushing her face against the mirror, telling her that's what a whore looks like. And when you noticed me, you didn't even stop.

Uncle Dee and Aunt Layla have no clue about what went on in our home, and if they truly knew, you wouldn't even have been able to stay here. When you left us with no money or food, what did you think would happen? I watched my mother transform from a vibrant, loving person into someone unrecognizable. You would come by every so often, and I thought you were there to rescue us, but instead, you just reveled in our suffering.

Keith, I completely understand how tough this is for you. Remember when Grandma Stacy passed away? It hit our family hard because she was deeply loved by everyone, especially by our daughter, Deedee. When Grandma left us, Deedee was just eight years old, struggling to grasp that she wouldn't see her again. Initially, we thought time would ease her pain, but as it turned out, she started showing signs of depression that needed our attention. Her teacher even called us in for a conference, concerned about Deedee's emotional state because she would cry unexpectedly.

After discussing our concerns with her teacher, she suggested creating an open space for Deedee to express her feelings while we shared our own. This recommendation was challenging, especially since we were still grappling with our own heartache over losing Grandma, and we weren't sure how to convey that to an eight-year-old. Layla and I took time to reflect on what we would say and noticed that we hadn't even mentioned Grandma's name since her passing. It felt like we were each dealing with our grief in our own isolated ways.

So, we made a pact to talk about Grandma amongst ourselves first, and then when we felt ready, we would bring Deedee into the conversation. There were moments of pure joy as we reminisced. One memory that cracked us up was when she burst out of her room wearing a makeshift costume. She looked both ways and dashed toward the door. We were completely bewildered, and just as she placed her hand on that door, she turned to us and, realizing something was off, said, today isn't Halloween, right.

With laughter bubbling up, Layla said, you're a week early. As she headed back to her room, she turned and said, next week we're gonna run, right? That cracked us all up, I was laughing so hard I had to sit down. And from that moment on, every time she saw us that week, she would say something like, I hope you're ready. or I'm not waiting for you, so be prepared. She was so serious that by the end of that week, we seriously thought we would be running from our oppressors. What a fun week that turned out to be.

Not mentioning Grandma took away the chance to celebrate and cherish the incredible memories we had with her. When we finally started sharing Grandma stories with Deedee, she didn't say much at first. Then one day, out of the blue, she burst in and declared, Grandma was right.

At first, we didn't realize the significance of her words, so she said it again: Grandma was right. She shared that just before Grandma passed, she had visited Deedee and whispered that she was going away, but would be back. Well, she reassured us that grandma had come into her room the prior night and told her she was back.

Layla and I exchanged astonished looks, trying to process what we just heard without alarming her. Layla put her hand over her heart and said, you're absolutely right; I can feel her right here. After that beautiful moment, Deedee's sadness started to lift. I truly believe that what helped the most was us finally talking about Grandma together. So, no matter how difficult it might feel, sharing your pain for KJ's sake is also an important step in healing.

Layla and KJ stepped out of his room, where they had been quietly absorbing our conversation. With a gentle hand, Layla placed KJ by Keith's side and announced that it was time. They made their way into the kitchen, and we lingered at the door, eager to catch a glimpse of what unfolded next.

We heard Keith tenderly declare, I loved your mother. It was a poignant moment, and our hearts ached when we peeped in and saw tears cascading down KJ's cheeks. Keith continued, reassuring KJ that he would do anything to bring Maymay back. Though she was gone, he emphasized that KJ still had him, his father. We could see the conflict brewing within KJ; he seemed on the verge of voicing a storm of emotions, yet he hung his head low instead.

In that moment, KJ's thoughts swirled:

> *My father, you are my father now. My mother would have given anything to hear those words. In fact, she did. She sacrificed everything, dreams, friendships, her very life, hoping to hear those words from you. It feels like her love was overshadowed by your chaos. After you left, she turned to alcohol, sharing burdens with me that no child should ever have to bear. There were times I feared for my life. Why did you turn our world upside down?*

As KJ focused, Keith shared,

> Son, when I met your mother, we were just kids, younger than you are now. Her family lived right next door.

KJ's inner voice interjected again:

> *You grew up alongside her, yet you saw her as the villain? Now this is getting really confusing.*

Your mother was a remarkable person. I remember sitting on the porch when she approached me to introduce herself. I can still vividly recall us running around, laughing and playing in our front yards. Your mom, your uncle Dee, and I were inseparable. When one of us was around, the other two weren't far behind. As we matured, people wondered who she would eventually marry. Although we all spent time together, I believed that she and I had a special bond. I thought I'd be the one fortunate enough to marry her.

KJ's thoughts responded:

Ha, Lucky for whom?

After a while, Keith emerged from the kitchen cradling KJ, who had drifted off to sleep during their talk. He laid KJ back in his bed and returned to the living room. Just as he settled down, he heard a rustle; KJ was shifting, revealing that he wasn't fully asleep, just trying to escape the moment.

> You know, he said, I found it much easier to talk to him than I imagined. In fact, it felt wonderful. I truly believe this marks the start of a positive relationship for us. I'm optimistic that we will be able to rebuild our lives together, and I can't wait to hear his sweet voice again.

I smiled at Keith but reminded him, that, that part may seem easy now, but please don't underestimate the depth of KJ's feelings. When he starts to share his memories, it might get complicated. I once repressed a difficult memory about Grandma that resurfaced during a conversation. When I learned she would be moving in with us, I was furious, and we argued about it for weeks. Oddly enough, it wasn't Layla who brought this up; it was Deedee, who reminded me, by saying, Daddy, you didn't even like Grandma. That hit hard.

All the joy and laughter faded in the wake of that startling reminder. KJ may have painful memories of his past with you, and I want you to be fully prepared for what may arise as he opens up. It's vital to approach this moment with love, understanding, and readiness to support KJ, no matter where the conversation leads.

> Thank you, Dee. It's critical for me to embrace honesty with him, and for the first time in quite a while, it's equally important for me to be straightforward with myself.

Layla wanted to know if Keith really understood what happened. He paused, lowering his head for a moment before lifting it again. You could see his eyes darting around the room, gathering his thoughts. Finally, with a glimmer of vulnerability, he looked at me, tears welling up in his eyes. He wanted us to know that he loved her. Layla yelled,

> What do you mean by that? If you truly loved her, I'm struggling to understand what went wrong between you two. Can you help clarify?

> When Maymay fell in love with Devell, and being her closest friend, she confided in me. One day, while we were sitting in our favorite spot by the boats, she asked me to guess what she was thinking. It was a game we enjoyed playing, so I took a shot. Are you thinking about the movie we watched yesterday? I guessed. She shook her head. Is it about riding the

boats? Again, she said no. So, I made one last guess. Is it about me?

When she responded, no, I'm thinking about how cute Devell is, it felt like a dagger to my heart. I remembered we were just around fourteen years old then. I confessed my feelings to her, and while she replied that she loved me too, it wasn't in the same way. Her exact words were, I love you like a brother. Those words stuck with me; I don't think I've ever truly moved past them."

I wondered why Keith and I hadn't discussed this earlier. I would have understood. We used to share everything. Why keep this from me?"

I felt embarrassed. By that time, I believed we were a couple. Once she revealed her feelings for Devell, our conversations shifted to revolve around him, and I found myself growing resentful. I realized I had lost her completely, and that awareness devastated me. The wild thing is, I never saw it coming. When she began dating him, it cut me deep. I had to mask how I felt about their relationship. I lost her as a girlfriend, but I held onto our friendship fiercely, not wanting to jeopardize that bond. I tried dating other girls, but my heart was still set on her.

There was this one day we were talking, and I finally told her how I felt. To my surprise, she burst into laughter. She didn't take my feelings seriously, and I interpreted it as her being rude. Her laughter still echoes in my ears, along with the ache it caused. I held onto the hope that one day she'd realize what we could have had.

It seems essential for you to reflect on that because your actions toward her seemed like a way to retaliate for the hurt you felt.

Keith took a deep breath, nodding in acknowledgment,

That happened when we were children, besides I know she wasn't laughing at me. It was her way of showing she had no response to my statement.

Keith all I'm saying is you should think about it. You said even today you could hear her laughing, and feel the pain as if it was yesterday.

When she and I got together, I forgave her. I was the reason why they broke up. When Devell joined the Air Force, I thought it was my opportunity to win her over, so I went after her with a vengeance. I wasn't going to let anything stand in my way; besides I knew he didn't love her the way I did. When he wrote and told her he thought they should see other people, she was devastated. She wanted to write and tell him she loved him, and didn't want to see anyone else, but I convinced her not to, to give him time to think about what he wanted. In the meanwhile, I was the one who helped put the broken pieces of her heart back together.

I spent as much time as I could with her, we went to the movies, dinner, and sometimes we just sat at her house and watched television. One day we were sitting in the park having a conversation when she told me for the first time in our life that she loved me, and wanted to be with me. When she spoke those words, it was as if the world was lifted off my shoulders. I had wanted to hear her say those words since we were children. I told her I wanted to be with her too, and had been waiting to hear those magical words. She told me the reason Devell joined the Air Force was because she was pregnant, and they wanted to get married when he returned.

Layla yelled,

What, Maymay was pregnant in high school?

KJ thought,

What, do I have a brother or a sister?

Yes, she was carrying Devell's baby. She truly loved him, so it wasn't a surprise when she told me they had been sexually involved. However, the baby and the marriage were a shock. I knew she would have done anything for him. Two months after he left, she had a miscarriage, which is why he broke it off.

I have to admit that when she told me this, I wanted to rip his head off. But then I realized that if he hadn't left, I wouldn't be with her and wouldn't love her the way I did, so my anger was short-lived.

Layla asked if their parents knew what was going on.

Yes, they knew.

I could tell Layla was very uncomfortable with what Keith was saying. Keith looked at her and, sensing her unease, decided it was time to end the conversation. He stood up and said, sounds like KJ is up. I think I'll take him to the park. We can continue this conversation later. KJ stepped out of the bedroom, and Keith eagerly asked if he'd like to head to the park. However, KJ paused for a moment before turning back into the room. I noticed a flicker of disappointment in Keith's expression as he watched him go. With a gentle smile, Keith told us he would be back in about an hour, giving us an opportunity to collect our thoughts. Layla and I sat together, absorbing the moment, when I thought I caught faint voices coming from KJ's room. Curious, I stood up and went to check, but the moment I opened the door, the voices stopped. KJ was sitting quietly on his bed, looking lost in thought.

Once back in the living room, I heard the whispers again, so I turned to Layla and asked if she could hear them too. She shook her head, so I ventured back to his room, and once more, the sounds ceased. I couldn't help but wonder what was going through his mind as he sat there with tears glistening in his eyes.

In his own world, KJ's mind was likely filled with emotions:

I'm so frustrated, why can't things just be different?

Returning to the living room, I noticed Layla was deep in contemplation about Keith's earlier remarks regarding Maymay.

> I can't believe what he said about Maymay. We were such great friends. There's no way she'd hide something this significant from me. We shared everything. She even told me about the time you kissed her.

> It was a long time ago, and we weren't together then, Layla. There's really no reason for her to mention it.

> I know that, but we shared everything.

> Layla, I promise what he shared is true.

> What? So, you knew about this and didn't tell me all these years?

> I didn't learn about it until Devell spoke to me right before he moved away. He shared that story, as well as the one about him and Keith being brothers. The story Keith just told is the same one Devell told me,

so I believe it. Devell thought Maymay would tell you after they got married, but since that didn't happen, it seems she chose not to.

I had no idea they were intimate. What else could she have kept from me?

Layla, I don't think it was about hiding anything. Given how things turned out, she may have just felt overwhelmed and needed to push those feelings aside.

But we were so close, how could she not share such a heavy emotion with me? We were practically sisters.

I could see how deeply this news affected her. My heart went out to her, and I walked over to wrap her in a comforting hug. I wished I could ease her pain, but I knew that answering her questions would take time, patience, and understanding. It reminded us both that sometimes, even the closest friendships can hold hidden layers we don't fully grasp, and that's okay. What matters is the honesty we share in this moment, and the support we can give each other moving forward.

Chapter Twenty

The following morning, Layla and I settled into the living room, enjoying some television time together, when I suddenly thought I heard a strange noise coming from the back of the house, the same unsettling sounds from the night before. Intrigued, I felt a surge of curiosity and decided to investigate. I peeked out the door, hoping to catch a glimpse or hear the source of the noise, but to my disappointment, all I found was silence. I waited for a moment, convinced that the sounds would return, but still, there was nothing. Just as I was about to head back to the living room, the sounds erupted again, louder this time, almost as if someone were desperately calling out. It didn't seem like Layla was picking up on this at all, and I began to question the reality of what I was hearing.

Noticing my anxiety, Layla asked me what was going on. With sincerity, I explained that the sounds were back and becoming increasingly clear. I expressed my confusion as to why she couldn't hear them, detailing how it seemed like a chorus of voices, now emanating from KJ's room. Once I said those words, my heart raced as I dashed down the hallway to check on him, finding him sitting quietly on his bed, appearing emotionally distant. I couldn't help but wonder what thoughts were swirling in his mind. It was then that Keith joined us, confirming that he too had experienced similar eerie voices coming from KJ's space.

Layla decided to extend her support to KJ, opting to sit right in front of him and gaze into his eyes, hoping for some connection. KJ, she began softly, I love you so much, and I'm so happy you're here with us. I know you miss your mom, and I really miss her too, she was such a wonderful friend to me. While she's watching over us, I hope she knows how much it saddens all of us to see you like this. I would love to hear just one word from you, anything to let me know you can hear me.

He seemed to look right through her, and after a moment of silence, she decided to head for the door. Just as she turned, she heard a soft voice,

Why did you leave me?

She paused, intrigued and hopeful, and repeated, what did you say? But, as she looked back, there was no visible sign of emotion from him, and she left the room, still pressing on for some clarity.

> *Why did you leave me? I begged you to stay or take me with you. Why did you leave me? I hate you; I hate you; I hate you,*

Layla returned to the living room, telling me about what she thought she heard just as she exited his room. It struck us that there might be something more to KJ's silence than we understood. I told her if she really heard him, perhaps she was the key to helping him open up. With determination, Layla decided to give it another shot, this time, to respond directly to his question. She walked back into his room and sat beside him, ready to connect.

> KJ, you asked me why I left you. I want you to know that I didn't want to go; it was something beyond my control.

As if he were recalling a memory, he closed his eyes and tilted his head toward the ceiling.

> *I remember that day clearly. My mom told me you would be coming to get me. I was overjoyed because I knew I would finally feel safe and loved. As soon as the car pulled up, I couldn't contain my excitement. I dashed past Mom, almost knocking her over, with a heart full of hope. I sprinted out the door, hearing her voice call after me: Be a good boy. I promised myself, 'I will be the best kid so you'll always want*

me with you. At the park, I felt like a new person. I ran, I played, I laughed more than I had in ages. But when it was time to go, the silence in the car weighed heavily on my heart. I feared that maybe you had changed your mind about taking me with you. When I looked into your eyes as I got out of the car, I wished you could feel all the joy and anxiety I was experiencing, but it felt like you didn't understand at all. I remember asking you, how can a six-year-old be expected to take care of a mother? It was a cry for help, and yet, you drove away without looking back. Watching the car disappear into the distance, I was filled with dread about what would come next.

It seemed like he was beginning to relax. Layla felt a wave of connection in the air. She leaned in and asked what are you thinking about?

No matter what anyone else might say, I hold a deep belief that my mother loved me. There were times when she would leave for days at a time, and in the beginning, it filled me with fear and uncertainty. But as time passed, I learned to cope with her absence, holding onto the hope that she would return to me. And when she did, her vibrant spirit shone through, even if that warmth sometimes faded all too quickly.

Layla stared in KJ's eyes

I wish I could understand what's going on in your mind. If only you would open up to me, I truly believe

I could be of help. Leaving you behind was not an easy choice; perhaps you can't grasp it now, but taking someone else's child without their consent is simply not something we can do.

My mom told me that I could move in with you, she really did, but it felt like a heartbreaking theme I've grown too familiar with: a longing for connection, yet sensing reluctance in your heart, similar to how my father turned away from me.

When Layla noticed a tear rolling down KJ's face, her nurturing instincts kicked in and she enveloped him in a warm hug.

I remember the time the police brought me to your house. You had assured them that it was your wish for me to stay, filling me with hope once again. But eventually, that hope was extinguished as I was sent back. How could you do that to me? You say you love me, but if that's what love looks like, I feel the need to distance myself from it. You were aware of what I was going through; you witnessed the chaos in our home when my mother was overwhelmed by her struggles, yet you still chose to leave. I was craving love, connection, and a sense of safety. Every time I reached out to you; it felt like my hand was pushed away. Why would this time be any different? This time, I refuse to be deceived; I recognize that this situation is likely temporary.

Just as Layla stepped out of KJ's room into the living room, Keith came in from outside, and the tension in the air was palpable. They settled into the living room, the smooth notes of jazz playing in the background. I could see that Layla was feeling frustrated and overwhelmed by everything. When I asked her what was on her mind, she expressed concern about whether Keith had taken KJ to see a doctor, believing there was something significant affecting him. Keith replied, yes, I've consulted several doctors, and they assure me he's okay. With time, he'll find his voice; I just need to be patient.

I understand that, but...

Layla interjected, struggling with her concern.

But what more can I do? I wish I could hear him call me Daddy again. Perhaps I'm just facing the consequences of my past actions toward his mother.

Layla, feeling a surge of emotion,

It's not you who's facing the consequences; it's KJ, he's the one who can't speak; he's the one feeling unable to live fully. He's just a boy, and it feels like he's given up hope.

Layla, I understand your frustration. I would give anything if I believed it would improve his life.

In softening her tone slightly, Layla replied,

We get that. It's not about placing blame here; it's about understanding him. What happened with Maymay is why he is hurting like this. Accepting that reality is the first step toward helping him. I'm trying to empathize with you, I truly am. If you can help me understand your perspective, perhaps we can figure out how to support KJ together. For heaven's sake, she loved you,

Keith's voice quivered with emotion

And I loved her too.

How could you claim to love her while doing what you did? What kind of person does that? After her passing, you didn't express sorrow; all you talked about was having a son. After the funeral, it felt like you handed me off to Fran as if she could replace my mother.

Layla could see the turmoil within Keith and spoke again,

How could you genuinely love someone and treat them the way you have? It just doesn't make sense. If you truly loved her, your actions would reflect that love. Her passing might have brought an end to her struggles, but it doesn't change the pain we all felt during that time. We all played a part in the family dynamics. If the truth had been laid out on the table, we could have had a different ending. Instead of pointing fingers, we could have supported each other through the challenges and sought a brighter path together. I can't help but wish that you'd found a way to express those feelings earlier. It would have made such a difference. I genuinely want to move forward.

As we sat there, it felt like a surge of emotion flooded through the room. It was a moment that caught us both off-guard. Keith's frustration was palpable, and it seemed like he was carrying years of unaddressed pain and confusion. Keith shot back,

I hated her, are you happy now? Is that really what you wanted to hear from me?

In a surge of anger, Layla stood tall and yelled for Keith to get the hell out of her house, and if he thought he was taking KJ with him, he was completely mistaken. I was taken aback by her strong response, it was a side of her I hadn't seen before, and it showed her fierce loyalty. He was about to leave, but I couldn't let him go without digging deeper because I needed clarity. I asked him what on earth made him develop such animosity towards her. He lowered his head and quietly admitted, I hated her because she died.

Layla leaped to her feet again, not believing a word he just said.

No way, that's unfair, you can't blame her demise on her, you know it's more complicated than that.

As Keith paused at the door, I sensed he was grappling with some heavy revelations. Then he shared,

> When I learned Devell was leaving the Air Force, fear gripped me. I didn't know how Maymay would react. The first time he visited, I saw the spark in her eyes, she still had feelings for him. We talked later, and although she said it was merely history, I couldn't shake the unease that settled in.

But Keith, she cherished you above everything else.

> No, he replied with conviction. You didn't see how they connected.

> Are you saying Devell is the cause of all this? That feels like you shifting the blame again. I saw the joy you and she experience with KJ's arrival. It transformed your relationship, by that time Devell was back, so that can't be the problem. Look Keith, you need to uncover your true feelings. We're family, and honesty is the foundation of trust. How can you expect to find clarity when you're not able to be real with us, or even yourself? Look within: why the deep-seated resentment? Don't you realize that whatever it is that you have locked inside of you is affecting your relationship with your son?

Keith took a moment, visibly wrestling with his thoughts.

I really want to be honest, but whatever issues I have, seem to be buried so deeply that I can't connect the dots. It's confusing.

I felt it was crucial to drive home the point:

Keith, Maymay loved you with all her heart, it's vital for you to understand the whole situation. When you come to terms with that, it can open the door to understanding everything that transpired.

Layla decided she could use some fresh air and thought it might be nice to invite KJ along with her to the store. If Keith chose not to share his truth with us, that's on him. She couldn't bear the idea of pretending that everything was fine when it clearly wasn't. She went to his room and returned. I could tell something was off. She explained that when she asked KJ to join her, he just stared blankly at the ceiling. She went over to him and tried to hold his hand, but he pulled away. It was evident that he wasn't in the mood to go anywhere. Before she left, she cast a glance of frustration at Keith, who sat there with his head lowered. I felt at a loss, unsure of how to respond. It was apparent that Keith was struggling, and his internal battles seemed to linger in the air around us. He slowly lifted his head, his eyes darting around as if he were trying to unearth something buried deep within. Then, our eyes met, and it felt as though he was peering straight into my mind, absorbing my unspoken thoughts. I asked him if he was okay, but he remained silent, his gaze penetrating and distant. Feeling uncomfortable, I stood up and noticed he was now intensely focused on the wall, as if searching for something beyond it. I called out to him, but he stayed unyielding.

I moved closer and placed a hand on his shoulder, which startled him,

> Man, what's wrong with you? When did you get up? How are you standing right next to me? What's happening in this house? I think KJ and I should leave. I don't know what this is, but I'm not comfortable with it.

I told him to take a breath, and that I didn't mean to startle him; I only wanted to get his attention. It felt like he was somewhere else entirely. In a burst of energy, Keith leaped up and headed for the door. I asked him what about KJ? What's going to happen to him? He said he thought he would be happier with us.

> I have to go for both our sakes. Just let KJ know I love him and that I'll carry him in my heart forever.

And with that, he stepped back into the unknown, leaving a void behind. When Layla came home from the store, she took one look at me and immediately sensed something was off. I confided in her about Keith's emotional state and how he had left KJ with us. She walked over, wrapped her arms around me, and told me not to worry, that he would return."

That night, I had a vivid dream that Maymay was with me, revealing that it wasn't her who had passed away but rather

her twin sister. She spoke of an encounter with her sister, someone she had never met, during her time on the street. On the night of the accident, her sister had been taking KJ to Devell's house. Her life had taken a dark turn, leading her to let the world believe it was her who had died.

In my dream, I held her close and wept. I wasn't sure whether my tears were for her survival or the troubles she had brought into our lives. As I embraced her, a wave of emotion surged in me, and I heard Layla's voice nudging me to wake up. When I opened my eyes, she asked softly why I was crying. I shared the dream and how lifelike it had seemed.

The following morning, I reflected on the dream and the possibility of her having a twin sister, I vaguely remembered someone mentioning it during my childhood. Before long, these dreams became a frequent occurrence, vivid enough that I often couldn't discern whether I was awake or lost in sleep. Initially, I shared these experiences with Layla, but over time, they felt increasingly bizarre to me, leading me to keep them to myself.

Chapter Twenty-One

It had been two years since we last saw Keith when KJ's voice finally filled the air for the first time. For months, teachers had been suggesting that KJ needed to be in a school that was more tailored to his unique needs, but Layla remained optimistic. She believed that with time, he would shine through just like any other child and didn't accept the notion that he had a disability. The night before KJ spoke, Layla sat down with him, explaining that if he didn't start expressing himself, it might be necessary to consider transferring him to a different school. As she spoke, something remarkable happened, KJ was looking directly into her eyes. Unlike previous discussions, when he tended to gaze past us, this time he was fully engaged. When she asked if he understood, something she always did after sharing important messages, he shook his head. Layla felt a wave of hope; she knew then that he was on the verge of returning to us.

The next morning, we awoke to the most enchanting sound, a beautiful voice singing joyfully. Initially, we thought it was coming from the television; the melody was so mesmerizing. As we lay in bed, we realized the TV was off. Curious, we searched the house for the source, and it suddenly clicked that the beautiful voice was KJ's. Layla sprang out of bed, urging me to come and witness this incredible moment with her. When I stepped into the kitchen, I found her standing there, tears of joy streaming down her face, while KJ stood just a couple of feet away, singing, "Just a Closer Walk with Thee". We stood there, completely entranced by his voice as he sang. The beauty of his voice was like nothing we had ever experienced before. He turned his gaze toward us, singing even louder.

In that moment, Layla told KJ how much we loved him, and he joyfully echoed her words back to her. This was particularly special for Layla, as she had been singing that very song to him every night for the last two years. We all joined together in this beautiful song, and in that instant, I felt overwhelmed with love, knowing that KJ had truly returned to us. I also had this strong sense that Maymay was there with us in spirit, celebrating too. From that day on, KJ transformed into a vibrant, happy little man, having emerged from tough times with resilience. While he didn't often dwell on the past, it felt as though that moment of singing had marked the beginning of a wonderful new chapter in his life.

Because of his incredible talent, Layla decided to enroll him in singing lessons, and it wasn't long before he joined a gospel group. Every time KJ sang a solo, I was filled with chills, as if his voice transcended him, resonating deeply with everyone listening. Thinking back to his emotional state when he first came to our home, it felt like nothing short of a miracle to witness his transformation.

One day, after rehearsal, KJ hurried into the house and straight to his room, clearly upset and without a word. Layla followed closely behind, and looking at her face, I sensed something significant had unfolded. She stood still for a moment, and then the tears flowed. I approached her and wrapped my arms around her, wishing to ease her distress. I wanted to ask what had happened, but I knew she would share when she was ready. As I held her, I could feel her take a deep breath, and gradually, she began to relax. She sat down, staring at the floor before slowly lifting her gaze. The intensity of her stare felt almost as if she could see my very heartbeat. I asked, what had happened. She took a moment, placing her hand on her forehead. Just a shake of her head followed, and I turned to head toward KJ's room, hoping to get some clarity from him. Just then, she stopped me.

> Don't disturb him. I'll explain what happened. Just give me time; I'll be okay.

I settled in, waiting patiently for her to open up. Each time she attempted to speak, her tears began anew, making the suspense almost unbearable. Then she said,

247

Today at rehearsal, I saw her.

Saw who?

I saw her... and KJ knows that I saw her.

Saw who? Please tell me who you saw,

When KJ began singing early on, he mentioned that he saw his mother every time he sang. I had been skeptical, thinking it was metaphorical, until that day when Layla described seeing her as plainly as the brightest sky. Layla said, she was there, watching him sing.

I can understand why he would think he saw his mother, but you too?

I'm telling you; she was there...

Are you saying you saw her spirit?

No, she was there in the flesh.

Now you're really scaring me,

Layla said, when KJ told her he saw Maymay in church, she thought he meant an angel. But he insisted it was his mother. This morning, while he was singing, he pointed to the back of the church, and when she turned to look, there she was. When she realized Layla saw her, she jumped up and ran out. Layla leapt up and followed her, but by the time she reached the door, she was already driving away. she was certain it was her. I thought they both was losing it, but it made me think of my dream, Maymay telling me she had a twin. I reminded Layla that she was at the funeral.

I know I attended her funeral, but what I saw was real. If it wasn't her, why did she run away?

I don't know, but this all seems too surreal to me.

We have to uncover the truth because I can't just let this go. I know what I saw, and I know she saw me. I'm going to New Orleans to talk to her family because angels don't drive cars.

Layla, KJ needs you here; I'll head down there to see what I can find out.

But you don't believe me...

I believe you saw something significant; I truly do. If KJ saw what you saw, he will need you close during this time. I'll go down there on Friday for a couple of days to gather some information."

That week, Layla and KJ interacted in hushed tones, at least when I was around. It was evident that their bond had strengthened through this shared experience, which was heartening to see, but it did leave me feeling a bit distant, as though I were an outsider to their extraordinary connection.

Their story inspired me to fantasize about the possibility of Maymay having a twin sister, maybe that was the mysterious figure they both encountered. The uncertainty was daunting as I prepared for my trip to New Orleans. The night before I was set to leave, sleep eluded me. As I lay there, I felt my heart racing. In an instant, a pang shot through my chest, and I struggled to reach out for Layla but found myself unable to move. Thankfully, over time, the pain eased, leaving me anxious yet resolved to uncover the truth.

Chapter Twenty-Two

I arrived in New Orleans late Friday night, filled with a mix of excitement and confusion. After several unsuccessful attempts to connect with anyone, I decided to check into a hotel. That night, I tossed and turned, trying to piece together why I was here. At home, this trip felt like an incredible adventure, but now it seemed overwhelming. What was I meant to do or say to the people I would meet? The thought of retreating home, crossed my mind, where I could tell Layla that I hadn't uncovered anything to support her hope that Maymay was alive.

The next morning, a knock on my door jolted me from restless sleep. Peeking through the peephole, I was astonished to see her standing there. I actually took a step back, doubting my senses, could this be a dream? But when I opened the door, she floated in like a character straight out of a storybook, confirming that this encounter was very real. She introduced herself as Alice, Maymay's twin sister. We settled down to talk, and she shared her heartfelt story with me.

Alice revealed that their mother had placed the twins for adoption, each with a different family, a decision that would shape their lives in unexpected ways. It wasn't until her eighteenth birthday that she found out about Maymay. Curiosity ignited within her, propelling her to search for her sister, though her efforts proved fruitless. Despite this, she carried Maymay in her thoughts as she continued to live her life.

At nineteen, Alice married and soon after became pregnant, but a devastating miscarriage three months in, left her heartbroken. This loss sent her into a dark depression, straining her marriage as she resisted her family's suggestions for counseling. However, when she discovered she was expecting twin girls, she felt an undeniable urge to reconnect with her sister. Driven by hope, she left her family behind and moved to New Orleans, certain that was where Maymay was living.

In New Orleans, Alice experienced surreal moments where strangers seemed to recognize her. This made her feel like she was getting closer to her sister. One remarkable day, while standing on a corner, she spotted a car with a driver who looked just like her. Time froze as both women stared in shock. The driver appeared equally astonished, and as the car passed, it almost got into an accident. Alice rushed to the corner, hoping to catch a glimpse again, but the car vanished. She stayed there for hours, yearning for a reunion that felt just out of reach.

But after that encounter, sleep became elusive for Alice. Everything around her felt increasingly surreal. Time seemed to slow down, and when people spoke, it felt as if they were conversing in a language she didn't fully understand. Houses appeared to fly by her in a blur, and there were stretches of time that slipped away, leaving her in unfamiliar surroundings, surrounded by strangers who seemed to know her while she grappled with her own identity.

Just as she was expressing this whirlwind of thoughts, another knock rang at the door. In a moment of instinct, she floated over, opened it, and let out a scream that echoed through the room.

Startled, I leapt out of bed, trembling and sweaty, unsure of what I had just witnessed. Immediately, I called Layla, eager to share the vivid details of my dream and the raw intensity that felt alarmingly real. A part of me knew it was just a dream, yet the experience felt so profoundly genuine that I found myself questioning that certainty. Layla chuckled, reminding me that it was just a dream, after all, people don't float around, right?

Still, I couldn't shake the feeling that there might be something deeper at play in this adventure, and I was eager to see where it would lead.

After my conversation with Layla, I tried my best to drift back into sleep, but it felt like an impossible task. I found myself pacing around the room, repeatedly reminding myself that I was merely caught in a dream, yet deep down, a part of me felt an undeniable pull, convinced that this was somehow real. As I walked, memories from my childhood swirled around me, almost as if my past was reaching out to share something important. Confusion washed over me, but instead of resisting, I decided to embrace the mysterious sensations clouding my mind. Just then, a chilly breeze swept through the room, sending shivers down my spine. Seeking warmth, I wrapped a blanket around my shoulders and headed to the thermostat, only to discover it read a toasty eighty-five degrees. Bewildered, I returned to the bed, wrestling with the overwhelming feelings swirling within me.

As I sat there, my eyelids grew heavy, and just then, a vivid vision surged into my mind. I could see myself as a child, standing outside my parents' bedroom door, listening to them discuss the terrible accident. They spoke of their fear regarding our close bond, worried that it could lead to romantic feelings and ultimately reveal the truth: that she and I were siblings. The weight of that recollection was incredible; it felt both shocking and disorienting. My thoughts seemed untrustworthy, leaving me in a greater state of confusion.

Just then, a loud pounding echoed at the door, as if someone were trying to break it down. I sprang to my feet, realizing I was caught in yet another dream. A wave of fear washed over me, and I felt like I was teetering on the edge of losing my mind. Hesitant about peering through the peephole, I feared what, or who, might be waiting for me. Gathering my courage, I crept to the door and looked through. And there she was, standing on the other side, her angelic smile lighting up the moment.

I desperately tried to reach for the door handle, but my arm felt like it was glued in place. I stood frozen, staring at the door, willing my arm to move, but nothing happened. Panic enveloped me; the more I strained to break free, the more paralyzed I felt. Before I knew it, I began to float away from the door. It was as if time sped up. When I looked back, the door appeared to be miles away. Finally, I found myself standing just a foot from the door. As the knob started to turn, I instinctively took a step back. In that moment, I understood, whatever was about to unfold was beyond my control.

Just as I placed my hand on the knob, I heard footsteps racing away, with my heart racing, I flung open the door and dashed into the hallway, calling out for the figure I saw sprinting around the corner. Stop, I yelled, but they just kept going. By the time I reached the end of the hallway, it was empty. Panic creeped in as I rushed back to my room only to find the door locked, I had forgotten my key. Turning toward the elevator to head to the front desk, the unexpected happened: the door swung open.

After getting a new key, when I opened the door, I was greeted by the sight of her sitting calmly on the bed.

Surprisingly, instead of fear, a sense of peace washed over me. I walked past her, keeping my gaze steady, and chose to sit at the desk near the window. An electric silence enveloped us. She looked so vividly real, yet I struggled to convince myself she was just a figment of my imagination. Driven by curiosity, I rose and slowly approached her, yearning to discover if I could touch her or if my hand would pass right through. When I placed my hand on her shoulder and stared into her eyes, disbelief coursed through me. To my astonishment, my hand connected with her, the sensation was unmistakably real. I fully anticipated waking from this bizarre experience, but the moment lingered on. All I felt was an inexplicable connection to her, as if the universe was guiding this encounter.

Suddenly, a wave of dizziness washed over me, and I instinctively gripped her shoulder tighter to regain my balance. The next thing I recall is waking up again, and I must admit, it was starting to frustrate me. I was caught in this strange limbo where I couldn't quite tell if I was living reality or drifting through a dream.

As I lay in bed pondering this, the phone rang, and a mix of excitement and apprehension surged through me. I paused, unsure of what, or who, might be waiting on the other end. After what felt like ages, I decided to answer. I held my breath silently, curious to see who had called.

Hello, Dee, are you there? came the familiar voice.

Layla, it's so good to hear from you. You wouldn't believe the whirlwind of events I've been through in the past few days," I could hardly contain my enthusiasm.

What are you talking about? You've only been gone for a day, she exclaimed, puzzled.

Before I could reply, a loud banging interrupted us, sending my heart racing. I shot upright in bed, exclaiming, what on earth is happening? In an instant, the door swung open, and nurses rushed in, expertly guiding me back down to the bed.

Sir, please stay still. You're going to be just fine. Just relax, one of them reassured me with a calm, soothing tone.

As I lay there, I couldn't shake the feeling of uncertainty. Was this all another dream, or was I truly in a hospital?

My eyes fluttered open, and I scanned the room, striving to piece everything together. Gradually focusing, I spotted figures moving around me, nurses, they were conversing, and it was clear their attention was on me. I tried to sit up, but a glance at my body revealed wires and tubes connected to my wrist and chest. I was surrounded by care, and I was determined to understand and overcome whatever lay ahead.

Chapter Twenty-Three

Reflecting on my life has truly opened my eyes to how I arrived at this point. The memories of my youth, Maymay, Devell, and the challenging times with Keith, have all resurfaced, and they hold more meaning than I ever realized. As I began to open up about these experiences with Layla, she excitedly interjected with some incredible news. She had reached out to her aunt, who was familiar with our families, and she revealed something astonishing. She asked me if I knew that Maymay had a twin. I responded, feeling a rush of emotions begin to swirl, is that who I've been talking to. is her name Alice. Layla continued, her eyes gleaming with excitement.

Wait a minute, there's even more. Maymay was adopted.

My heart raced as the pieces of a long-unfinished puzzle began to connect. Glancing at Layla, it was clear she had much more to share. She said, Dee, you were also adopted. I was taken aback. What? Layla, are you serious?

Yes, it's true, they never told you, but it's a fact.

My mind was spinning. This just doesn't make sense. How could I not have known?

Hold on, there's more.

What do you mean? Are you saying Maymay and I are siblings?

Exactly, and twins.

A wave of emotions crashed over me, momentarily overwhelming my senses. For an instant, panic gripped me as I feared this was just another wild dream. But Layla continued, explaining that the twin I had dreamt about was indeed me. Tragically, our biological parents had passed away in a car accident, and we had been separated, living right next to each other without any clue that we were related.

As the reality settled in, I felt weak. The next thing I remember, I was lying in bed, and Layla had stepped away. When she returned, I couldn't contain my questions.

Is it true? Maymay and I are really siblings, twins?

With a warm expression, she confirmed it again, and I couldn't help but reflect on our childhood. Maymay always felt incredibly special to me, and the bond we shared now took on profound meaning, if only we had known earlier.

Driven by a mix of hope and determination, I made some calls to uncover the truth. When my mother confirmed the news, everything clicked into place. Those dreams I had been perhaps Maymay's way of reaching out to me, expressing our deep connection. Suddenly, my grief over her loss transformed; I wasn't just mourning a friend, but the absence of my twin sister.

Understanding Maymay's situation helped me empathize with Keith's feelings when he discovered Devell was his brother. He was fortunate to have a chance to build a relationship.

With this newfound knowledge, we decided to gather and address the family secrets that had clouded our pasts. Keith, with sincerity in his voice, began to share his thoughts on how he had treated those close to him. After extensive therapy and soul-searching, he came to some enlightening realizations.

> It wasn't only about Maymay, KJ, or Devell, I had so many unprocessed emotions hidden away that I wasn't even aware of. The first was the strain in my relationship with my father; I felt abandoned. I walked away from my job, determined not to let it define me. Then, my mother internalized her pain

261

instead of communicating it, leading to the unraveling of our family. When I thought Maymay and Devell were together, those buried emotions resurfaced, subconsciously guiding my actions. It felt like I was an outsider. But I've come to realize my father didn't abandon me, my mother wasn't angry with me, and my wife loved me all along.

With openness and hope in his heart, Keith expressed his desire for us to forgive him, and he yearned to find that forgiveness for himself one day.

This journey of discovery has not only deepened our understanding of one another but has strengthened our bonds, filling me with optimism for what lies ahead.

Keith and KJ gradually began to rebuild their relationship in such a heartwarming way. When Keith first arrived at the house, their interactions were minimal, and conversations were strictly cordial. Keith made it a point to check in with KJ about his feelings and his day at school, but initially, KJ responded with only a few words. One transformative day, KJ confronted his father with a poignant question: "Why did you hate Mom so much? Although Keith had been skirting around discussions about his past behavior, KJ's question forced him to confront the issue. With sincerity, Keith explained that he didn't hate his wife; rather, the real challenge lay in his own inability to love himself.

KJ had been carrying the heavy weight of believing he was the root of his mother's unhappiness, thinking that if he had never been born, she wouldn't have to endure suffering. Keith took the opportunity to reassure his son that this notion was far from the truth. He emphasized that KJ was, in fact, the brightest spot in his mother's life, the blessing that had kept her motivated to turn her life around. That heartfelt conversation marked the beginning of a significant shift, allowing Keith and KJ to forge a stronger bond.

Keith had the intention of inviting KJ to move in with him, but to his surprise, KJ respectfully declined, expressing that he was happy where he was. It was clear that KJ was coming into his own and recognizing his own sense of stability.

As I reflected on my relationship with Maymay, a deep curiosity surfaced about our origins and where our story began. Eager to uncover the truth, I reached out to my mother, who filled me in on some incredible details about our past. She shared that the adoption agency that had helped us was no longer in operation, and reminisced about the heartbreaking accident that had unfolded right before her eyes. My mother was the one who bravely pulled us from the wreckage just moments before it exploded. She and Maymay's mother, both moved by our plight, made the decision to take us in when no one else came forward. They had always meant to share our story with us but never found the right moment. She encouraged me to visit the library and look up twin Babies Rescued from Burning Car.

The search for that article took time, but when I finally found it, I was astonished to spot Nurse Vanassa in the background of the photograph. It felt surreal. Although I knew it was a long shot, I felt compelled to speak with her to uncover what she might know.

I decided to keep my findings from Layla until I had more clarity. I headed to the hospital, only to discover that Nurse Vanassa had retired right after I had left. I was disappointed but remained determined, convinced she held a vital piece of the puzzle regarding our family. Weeks passed, and despite my best efforts, I struggled to uncover more leads. Just as I was about to lose hope of ever finding them, a twist of fate occurred. I spotted Nurse Vanassa leaving the local grocery store, and disbelief washed over me.

A rush of excitement mixed with nervousness enveloped me as I stood beside her, feeling a sensation that was both exhilarating and surreal. I wanted to speak to her, but something held me back. It felt almost dreamlike, and then I heard a calm voice reminding me, you are not dreaming; I'm here.

Following her lead, we ventured to a cozy coffee shop where she opened up about my family. To my astonishment, I learned that I had another sister, and her name was Alice. This moment felt like the beginning of a beautiful new chapter, filled with hope and possibilities.